EMRE Publishing, LLC
presents

SERENE

BY

Jim Musgrave

Dr. Rachel E.

Color-Me-a-Mystery, Number 1

DEDICATION

To the power of imagination, whose magic allows the poor to see beyond their poverty, and whose trajectory sends us throughout the universe.

EMRE Publishing, LLC is a publishing house based in San Diego, California. Website: emrepublishing.com

For more information, please contact:

English Majors Reviewers and Editors, LLC
6784 Caminito del Greco San Diego, CA 92120-2219
publisher@emrepublishing.com

ACKNOWLEDGMENTS

I want to thank my editor, Lynda Rucker, who was recently awarded the prestigious Shirley Jackson Award for her short story, "The Dying Season." Congratulations, Lynda, and may some of your good vibrations rub off on my mystery series the way Aladdin could rub his lamp. Speaking of genies, I also want to give kudos to Amanda Fedric, who was able to make some of my wishes come true by creating the fun coloring book illustrations for this mystery. Bai Ilando, an excellent Japanese artist, did the front cover illustration that can be colored.

And, once again, I want to thank all those creative scientists and engineers out there who are inspiring many of the inventions that I discuss in this book. I cut my scientific research teeth at Caltech, and I am forever indebted to all the creative imaginations of great minds from the trades and disciplines around the world. I do lament the fact that the powers in academia are drifting away from teaching literature to our students. The greatest scientists and engineers that I have known were all extremely literate, and they enjoyed science fiction the way one enjoys a fine wine. Fiction helps students find their analytical wings and allows them to fly high, without a net of facts tying them to the ground. My favorite quote that I used quite often in my English classes came from Soichiro Honda, CEO of the Honda Corporation: "Success represents the 1% of your work which results from the 99% that is called failure." Reading and discussing literature allows our students to make mistakes without the glaring tag of "failure" being forever affixed to their attempts.

In addition, the natural empathy that exists in all humans is best strengthened through the free imagination experience that only the Arts can bring. In fact, one of my favorite authors, Albert Camus, once said, "Without freedom, no art; art lives only on the restraints it imposes on itself, and dies of all others." Art, in today's *realpolitik*, is dying because of the fear of our Cowardly New World to accept controversy as a necessary ingredient of real argument. A lot is being bandied about by leaders concerning the ability to "walk in the shoes of another" in order to cure bigotry and racism. The best way to learn how to do this is to provide the literature that shows this better than any non-fiction essay I've ever read. Any creative writer worth his sodium began writing stories because of the "what if?" What if I woke-up one morning and I was an insect instead of a human? What if the world were being ruled by countries that manipulated non-fiction "news" in order to make their leaders seem all-powerful? If writers hadn't been able to flex their empathetic muscles, we would not have *The Metamorphosis* by Franz Kafka or *1984* by George Orwell.

SERENE

Other works by Jim Musgrave

Non-Fiction
The Digital Scribe: A Writer's Guide to Electronic Media

Fiction
Det. Pat O'Malley Historical Steampunk Mysteries:
Forevermore
Disappearance at Mount Sinai
Jane the Grabber
Steam City Pirates

Lucifer's Wedding
Sins of Darkness
Russian Wolves
Iron Maiden an Alternate History
Love Zombies of San Diego
The President's Parasite and Other Stories
The Mayan Magician and Other Stories
Catalina Ghost Stories

Contents

"In order to exist, man must rebel, but rebellion must respect the limits that it discovers in itself - limits where minds meet, and in meeting, begin to exist." Albert Camus

PROLOGUE: SID AND ROSE

Present day…San Marcos, San Diego County, California

When Dr. Joshua Lawrence used the brains of Doctors Sidney and Rose Edelstein, he knew they were Jews. In fact, since Lawrence had been raised to hate Jews by his parents in Santa Cruz, all of his scientific planning to bring about The Singularity was focused on creating a plan whereby Jews would be seen as the scourge of humanity, and so their eradication would be welcomed and not mourned.

In 1990, these two Jewish scientists were in charge of the research and development at Omshanti ashram when Dr. Lawrence began his work there. Dr. Lawrence made it his purpose in life to use Sid and Rose and their child Rachel to conquer the chaotic mess that was human society. Now that his plan had been changed, the back-up option was being carried out without Lawrence in direct control. Perhaps it was more fitting to have the final plan being instigated without Dr. Lawrence. After all, once The Singularity began, all biological humans would be radically changed to fit the correct world order.

There was only one major plan programmed into the two androids, and it was developed to be carried out even in the event of the death of the programmer. When Dr. Lawrence was murdered inside his lab, this program inside of Sid and Rose immediately went into action. The only reason this plan had not been initiated was that Dr. Lawrence sent the two androids secret WiFi signals each day to keep the secret plan in hibernation. As soon as this signal was not transmitted, Sid and Rose began to carry out Lawrence's ordered sequence of specific instructions.

Sid and Rose Edelstein looked and felt human. They were the ultimate androids, perfected by the latest computer, genetic, and robotic technology. One could tell Sid and Rose were not biologically human because the nervous system of a human is not perfectly wired the way theirs were. Therefore, Dr. Lawrence, their creator, was not able to perfect the idiosyncratic little tics and motions that biological humans projected. However, this was not necessary for this ultimate plan. Since Sid and Rose were technically the first Jewish androids, they would have advantages when they made their Aliyah to Israel.

The miracle of The Singularity was the ultimate goal. Sid and his wife could already connect with any computer by WiFi to process problems at speeds of up to 30 quadrillion bytes compared to the human brain at 3.5 quadrillion bytes. According to the most recent calculations, unless human society were taken over by machines, it would self-destruct in less than one hundred years.

Sid and Rose, at the moment, were being transported together as luggage across the Atlantic Ocean toward Israel. Their minds were off, so they could not process at the powerful speeds they soon would be during their assignment. However, even at rest, the potential was there, and their controller, who was reading and writing on a laptop in seat 42, row 6, on board El Al Flight 7513, knew that once the plan was put into motion, Sid and Rose would be the most valuable part of The Singularity puzzle.

Rachel

We made it out to the ashram in one piece, thank God, but we weren't prepared for the news we were greeted by once we arrived. I was planning ahead, so I bought the two El Al tickets to Israel through my smartphone. I argued with Jacob about paying the cost, but we agreed that it could become our first business expense, so I bought them on my card.

Linda Peterson was in Guru Sharma's office. She was the blonde candidate for bride of passion from my youth. She approached me with a concerned frown.

"Dr. Edelstein, we just received a call from Israel. It was the office of Mossad. They want you to visit them as soon as you touch down. They would only say the information they have is for your eyes and ears only. Also, we have been unable to track-down any flights that report having androids as part of their manifest of persons or luggage."

"Thank you, Linda. You may call me Rachel, by the way. Jacob and I have our tickets, and we'll get going shortly. If Mossad's getting involved, then you can bet your bagels there's some terrorist activity afoot. I hope they don't think we're suspect, but I'll let you know."

Guru Sharma looked much older and exhausted. As a girl, I remembered only his penetrating gaze and fluid motion. His gentle nature was still there when he spoke. "I often wonder if my karma has caused all of this trouble. I am going to assemble all members to pray for you, Rachel, and for Dr. Stein. You will be saving our reputation as a religious organization, and we are very grateful. Please keep us informed."

I walked over to him and took his two brown hands in mine. His sexual traumas glittered around him like messages of Ein Sof. In my frantic effort to use my new psychic ability, I had forgotten about my practice of Kabbalah. It wasn't about me or even about the ashram. It was about making certain the best interests of humanity, as a whole, were being protected.

"I will text you personally, Guru. Of course, if I'm forbidden to communicate what happens in Israel, then you'll know why I'm not messaging you. I do have one more question for you before we leave. Do you have an ashram in Israel?"

"Yes. I opened it in 2000 to celebrate the Millennium. I think we have about ninety-five members there. Dr. Yaron Levine is the Guru at our Tel Aviv location. We rent two floors at the Academic College at Yaffa, and the devotees live privately off campus."

"Did Dr. Lawrence ever go out there?" I was intrigued by this news.

"Yes, he did. He traveled there at least four times," said Guru.

"Thank you. I think I'll also pay a visit there while I'm investigating."

"I understand. May Lord Vishnu protect you both, and may Lord Shiva give you the courage to discover the guilty and punish them."

Later, as we took off from San Diego International to head for Tel Aviv's Ben Gurion International Yafo Airport, I looked over at my new partner, Dr. Jacob Stein, and smiled. "I think I can smell me a Professor Moriarty, my dear Watson," I said. "Also, I don't think it was a cartel member that put the hit on Dr. Lawrence."

"Oh yes? What makes you say that, Sherlock?"

"When we discussed robots cleaning up the crime scenes, I thought about my robot parents. I am also aware of how the IDF and the Israeli government in general do their business. I think the IDF finally found some hard evidence linking Lawrence to the murders. They also knew he was an American citizen, so the only way to bring him to justice was to do what they used to do to the Nazi war criminals who were hiding out in other countries after the war."

"You mean, they sent out the Mossad?"

"Right. For those guys, it would have been a piece of cake to terminate him."

"Shut up, and eat these goobers. I brought them for a nosh," he said and passed me his bag of peanuts.

PART ONE: IN OUR IMAGE

CHAPTER ONE: OMSHANTI

San Marco, San Diego County, California, 1992

Rachel

I can feel the rose oil on my skin. Mother Serene says that being chosen as the Bride of Passion is an honor. We who are candidates speak together about what it all means.

"The Guru selects the one who can bring Omshanti closer to alignment with our guiding galaxy." Elouise looks up at the blue sky as she says this. Her head is always in the clouds.

I have a more practical guess. "He likes young girls. I've seen him staring at my ass when we dance the Shiva and Shakti at the monthly full moon celebration."

"Rachel, you should be dancing as Kali, the menacing one. You are always seeing the darkest aspects of existence." Linda is jealous because I was chosen over her. We have always been rivals, but I am the one who got his stares, and I am the one who is to be his bride of passion.

All those girls who were not selected perform the ritual of preparation inside the passion chamber. I did this last year, when I was twelve, so I know what is done to the room where it all takes place. First, the water bed is layered with rose petals. I remember seeing the soft red tongues undulate like a crimson sea as I pushed down on the end of the bed.

Another girl sprays the room with lilac scent so it becomes a floral paradise of odors that mix with the burning frankincense-jasmine incense. The smoke curls from the black rods stuck inside the tusks of the statue of the Ganesha, the elephant-headed god of new beginnings. One girl climbs a ladder to clean the ceiling mirror, which has the characters of the Hindu Trinity pasted on it. Brahma, the Creator. Vishnu, the Preserver. Shiva, the Destroyer or Transformer.

Every bride enters the passion chamber to the recorded music of Ravi Shankar. Guru says that since we are all one family, our surname fits our nature. Serene is a state of calm joy, peaceful tranquility that can withstand the rigors of the outside world and the passions of the inside demons of temptation and fear.

However, as I enter the chamber, I do not feel serene. My heart is racing, and my palms and forehead are perspiring. No matter what my parents have told me about this ceremony, something inside me says it is not natural. Before we came to Omshanti, we lived together in Ocean Beach.

My parents are scientists. They work for Guru to develop technology that helps humanity. I might one day become a scientist, but right now I want a time machine to take me out of this room! My father said we were Jews, and my mother read me the Hebrew Scriptures every night before I went to sleep. It is one of those stories that fills my consciousness as Guru walks toward me inside the chamber.

Linda stands next to me as I recline on the bed, my perfumed body rippling on the waterbed like a lotus. She extends the red satin pillow to me. On it are the daily passion pills that are given to those girls who have had their first menstruation. I take one and place it on my tongue. I swallow, but my mouth is dry, so I gag.

Guru has a silver goblet in his hand, and he places the rim to my lips. I drink the dark blue liquid, and it is my first taste of wine. As he waves Linda away, I can hear her bare feet padding softly on the wood floor, and then the door shuts behind her. Guru says two words before my entire mind is taken over by my Jewish fantasy: "My bride."

I stand with my people on the top of Mount Masada in Israel. It is just after the Romans destroyed the temple in Jerusalem, and they were now coming after us. We know there is no hope. We are outnumbered. They have the weapons, the monstrous battering ram on the 300-foot platform. We can hear the wheels turning in the desert sand as the platform approaches the cliffs on the west side. There is only one way out because without suicide, we will be forced to worship their false gods.

Omshanti has taught me to worship false gods. And now, the tall dark man with the flowing beard is grabbing at my nightgown. I have no underwear. I have no escape.

I remember the quote from Josephus because we discussed it one night after my mother read it to me. I was told that the mystical meaning behind the quote was that we can only escape persecution by dwelling in the mystery of Yahweh's Kingdom:

"We must not choose slavery now, and with it penalties that will mean the end of everything if we fall alive into the hands of the Romans. God has given us this privilege that we can die nobly and as free Jews and leave this world as free Jews in company with our wives and children."

My passion is taken from me inside this chamber. As Linda cleans up the bloodstains on my legs and inner thighs, I come back to this world. I think about my parents coming to America.

My parents never spoke much about it. They were a part of the contingent of orphans allowed to immigrate to an abandoned Bronx YMCA in the summer of that year. My father came from Russia and my mother from Poland.

My mother told me there was a small staff of local Jews who welcomed the international contingent of children to this building in the hot summer of 1946. "Our receiving center in the Bronx was a dark multistoried structure, an absolute fire trap, with many small rooms and few bathrooms. Not a tree nor bush was in sight from the front stoop, we were surrounded by asphalt." My mother told me this when we lived in Ocean Beach. She said she was five years old and my father was seven.

My father never talked about anything related to these days. He was found by Russian troops abandoned in a field after the fleeing Germans had come through the night before, shooting every Jew they could round up. Somehow, one of the Russian peasants, a non-Jew, had taken him to this field and left him there.

Imagine waking up in the Tower of Babel every morning. These children came from Finland, Lithuania, Poland, Germany, and many other countries. They did not understand each other, nor did the American staff understand them. Their Jewish orthodoxy was as varied as their national origin, but a few spoke Yiddish. Even that language was of little help since each region of the world where it is spoken has developed a distinct dialect.

"We used hands, feet and facial grimaces to get our message across the language barrier. We played Jacob's ladder, a string game played by children all over the world, to establish a common ground with the other young people," my mother said.

The campers spanned the ages of one to officially eighteen, although they knew that some of the boys were older but were able to disguise their chronological age to qualify for a United States visa. The youngest child, found naked in a hayloft outside Kiev by a U.S. soldier, was estimated to be between one and two years old. "She came to the Bronx nameless, and we had a little naming party for her a few days after she arrived; we gave her the name Ruth, our director's name."

I loved to hear these stories from my mother. They were the only connections I had with my past other than our lives together as a tiny family of three. When my parents were able to graduate from college in New York City, which had very inexpensive tuition in those days, they got married. As they were both engineers, they had a lot in common, and they were even able to work at the same company, IBM. They were transferred to UCSD in 1969, where IBM was financing a computer research project.

When Guru Sharma came to San Marcos in 1990, he offered them a job. They had seen him in his orange robes in downtown San Diego. My parents worked on their own assisting the homeless on weekends. Sharma was building up his ashram in San Marcos, and when he told my parents about his belief in science and human freedom, they became his first converts from the professional research and development community. I was ten when we moved out of our house in Ocean Beach to the commune in San Marcos. I was twelve when I was chosen as the Guru's "bride of passion."

A boy named Seth runs up to me that day as I am walking back to our dormitory. His eyes are wide, and his voice trembles. "Your parents are dead! I saw them take their bodies out of the lab."

Guru

Bhagwan Sharma told them when they entered Omshanti that they were born anew. Just as he was able to come to America without the burdens of the past, so he presented his followers with a new way of seeing this world of illusions. The answer to this mysterious existence, where we attempt to become citizens of a country whose leaders believe military power is the only way to achieve respect, is to grasp local control over the body politic.

He began in 1990, with 208 followers, when the United States started its decline and was losing its center. He drove his Volkswagen van down Market Street, where the newly homeless could be found, and he recruited members for the new colony of Omshanti. He told them he would inspire them to think as one and to learn to work in gardens and laboratories in return for free food, guided meditation, and joyful dancing. He told them that the only way out of this nation that runs on the greed of the senses is to learn the ancient lesson of serenity.

With every new individual and family group that was brought to the rented compound in San Marcos, he was counting votes. He knew they would grow and survive only if they were able to vote enough members on the city council. All of his hopes and dreams of establishing a commune of scientific progress and spiritual harmony rested on whether or not they could gain control of that council form of government.

The date is May 21, 1992, and they have grown into a group that owns this ten acres of land with the fifteen buildings and the Omshanti Temple. They are now a 501c, tax-exempt religious organization with 875 followers. They are growing by an average of fifteen new members each week, and they recruit from other states and countries.

He now has a Rolls Royce instead of the damaged VW, and serenity permeates his every step inside Omshanti. As a licensed California pastor of the Hindu faith, he can perform marriages, which he does. However, all of the couples understand that their loving bonds are not trapped inside monogamous ritual. Instead, sexual love becomes just as important to their serenity as spiritual love. If they can share their possessions, even their wives, then they can share love on all levels of existence.

No longer does Omshanti become trapped inside the box of conformity and militant ritual. They dance, they sing, and they share joy, and they hope to keep their Andromeda Galaxy moving toward this Milky Way. Our planets have beings who share physical love and inner spiritual harmony, and Omshantians believe it is their purpose to grow in numbers so that when Andromeda finally mixes with Earth's galaxy, all humans will be prepared for the changes that will occur.

Until then, he can only create the serenity of passionate openness by initiating these brides of passion. The steps are exactly sixty-three from his room in the Serenity compound to the bridal suite. In Nepal, the living child Kumari goddesses are worshipped by Hindus and Buddhists. But they are prepubescent, and his goddesses must be women.

The power of his lingam can only be raised by entering a virgin yoni. It is, indeed, the left-handed Tantric method. His spirit is sated from this ceremony, and he does not prohibit homosexual or bisexual activities as a path to awaken the Kundalini snake inside. He only wants followers to show love and devotion toward others with whom they perform coitus.

He chose her because her parents were martyrs. She must learn that her love extends outward to encompass the universe, just as she has the universe contained within. Monogamous family constructs serve capitalistic masters. Not that having mistresses or misters is discouraged on the outside.

No, as long as the capitalists benefit from the sins, straying from the nuclear family is permitted. They must show them all how love is to be shared, just as wealth of mind and spirit must be shared. Her parents realized this, even though they died attempting to show the world how it can be possible to harness Eros to control violence.

She gags on the passion pill, so he gives her a drink from his chalice. He looks into her dark eyes and says, "My bride."

After he cleans up, he can see the boy running toward her on the quad. They must have come to collect the bodies. When she begins to scream, he knows her time with Omshanti is over.

CHAPTER TWO: YOU'RE IN THE ARMY NOW

Rachel

Tel Aviv, Israel, August 2014

It seemed I had left the Omshanti commune in San Diego only to enter another, more heavily armed, commune in Israel. When my parents died, Bhagwan Sharma told me he would provide for my education and welfare. He said that my parents died while working on a secret project that would allow humans to control the passionate desire within in order to prevent violent thoughts and actions without.

I later discovered the autopsies revealed they officially died from brain aneurysms caused by surgery. Sid and Rose Edelstein, from the Bronx, New York, became the first two martyrs to the Omshanti cause. I believed the key to my own childhood trauma might be found if I could determine what that project was they were working on.

True to his word, Guru Sharma supported my schooling through high school, onto undergrad and graduate work at UCSD, and finally, I received my medical degree in psychiatry in June, 2012. Most of my friends on the ashram attended my graduation that day, including our Guru, and as I looked out on the audience from the stage, I could see the wide patch of orange and red, signifying the official colors of Omshanti.

Guru Sharma told me I no longer had to live on the ashram, if I chose not to, but he hoped I would one day see that Omshanti represented the path out of the militant confusion that the world outside insisted was worth dying for. I had no other choice but to accept the Guru's offer of support, as I no longer had any family. My parents' relatives had died in concentration camps, so we were left without legal forebears, and our path to the commune became a way to find physical security and inner tranquility.

When I decided to enter the Israeli military, I had not established a therapy practice, and part of my motivation was to gain experience as a psychiatrist working with a country that I now considered "my people." When I traveled in August of 2012 to Israel as part of a free Aliyah, or Eretz Israel program, I immediately saw that my country needed me. I learned Hebrew in my training when I served in the Israeli Defense Forces.

SERENE

As a response to the weekly suicide bombings in public buses, public schools, and inside hotels and nightclubs in Tel Aviv, the walls were ordered to be built to protect Israel from the West Bank population of over 300,000 Palestinians. Indeed, before the completion of the first continuous segment in July 2003 from the beginning of the Second Intifada, 73 Palestinian suicide bombings were carried out from the West Bank, killing 293 Israelis and injuring over 1,900. After the completion of the first continuous segment through the end of 2006, there were only twelve attacks based in the West Bank, killing 64 people and wounding 445. Terrorist attacks declined in 2007 and 2008 to nine in 2010.

I guess Robert Frost was being ironic with his poem about "good fences making good neighbors," but to us Israelis, fences are a necessary burden on Palestinian transportation in order to prevent terrorist attacks. However, ever since Prime Minister Fleischman was elected and re-elected, the uproar from the World Court, Amnesty International, and other respected organizations has been louder against what they now call "the apartheid wall." The government has exacerbated the problem by allowing new Israeli settlements to be built inside Gaza under the guise of a new nationalistic view that sees all Palestinians as the enemy.

I stood at the Wailing Wall in Jerusalem when I decided to enter the IDF as an officer. It was 2012, and I had my dual citizenship. Linda from Omshanti had written to me the day before saying that their group now had over 3,000 members, and they owned many restaurants, stores and organic farms in the San Marcos area. "In fact," she said, "we had to get our own private police force because of the death threats coming from the citizens living in the community outside our ashram." I now understood that no matter where you lived, if you espoused a religious doctrine, you were going to have to fight to protect your freedom to be different.

Two years later, when over 4,000 rockets were fired into Israel from Gaza, Israel conducted a military operation in Gaza known as Protective Edge. The invasion into Gaza lasted 51 days in July and August 2014. It was the third major Gaza operation by the Israeli armed forces in seven years, and by far the most lethal and destructive. Some 2,205 Palestinians, including 722 militants and over 500 children, and 70 Israelis (64 of whom were soldiers) were killed. Thousands of Palestinians were wounded; over 18,000 of their homes were destroyed; some 470,000 were displaced, and large areas of Gaza were essentially razed.

I became a personal protective edge for the over 700 IDF victims of post-traumatic stress disorder, and I learned firsthand that my search for how and why my parents died inside the Omshanti lab had followed me around the world and into my office in Tel Aviv on that day of 21 August, 2014.

The patient I saw that day was Sergeant Seth Berman, 30, of the elite Golani Brigade. He was pale and stooped and completely bald as he sat on the couch inside my sparse military-style office on the nightclub strip in Tel Aviv. The IDF had set my office up in a haphazard manner inside the Haaretz Hotel, and my little room had a long blue couch, a scarred metal desk, and a three-wheeled padded green chair that kept rolling around under me as I listened to the young man's story.

I had given him my usual patient injection of 25mg of sodium thiopental combined with hypnosis. I have my certificate in therapeutic hypnosis, and I know that too much "truth serum" can lead to flights of fancy that are as far from the truth as one can get.

The combination of the two brought out the best results in my experience as a practicing psychiatrist. In fact, I personally use it to get from my office back to my IDF Officer's Quarters on the base nearby. I suffer from severe agoraphobia, or "fear of public spaces," and I need the drug to keep panic attacks at bay. I find that many Israelis also suffer from this disorder, and as terrorists increase their attacks, I expect I will see even more free-floating anxiety in the population at large.

Sergeant Berman began with his first-person narrative in Hebrew about the raid into Gaza, and I had heard many such stories over the weeks inside my office. It was near the end of his story, however, when he was beginning to come out of his trance, that I learned about how he was personally connected to me and to my own search for the truth.

He was acting out a scene from the apartment in Tel Aviv where he now lives with his mother, a nurse at the city hospital. As he spoke to me, his hands pantomimed his drug ritual, and he took from his pocket an article to read. He even danced, and when he was finished, I knew I had my own questions to ask him.

I place the bead of black tar on the spoon. The IDF gets me the best Mexican heroin government money can buy. I can see my reflection inside the silver spoon, one of my mother's kosher spoons for Passover. My upside-down, bald oval head looks like the 'alien head' Saul gave me one night in the barracks. He held his watch next to his shorts and asked me, 'Hey Seth, is this the right time?' and when I looked down I saw Saul's testicle, the alien head, sticking out from his shorts.

As I hold the needle inside my water bottle and watch it suck up the liquid into the syringe, which is also my diabetic mother's, I contemplate the irony of the fact that she is now providing me with more than the simple act of giving birth or nurturing my body. I add the water onto the spoon with the black bead, and it now looks like a little island of black hope, the only hope I now have left since the day I returned from Gaza.

I rolled into Gaza with my fellows. We all were laughing and joking about the girls we were with the night before inside a Tel Aviv dance club. Saul had ordered a bunch of chickpeas and told the girls to sit next to each other and open their mouths wide, like baby birds. He told them he was the 'world's best grenade launcher' and that he practiced by tossing garbanzo beans. Each one of the girls received a tossed bean in her mouth; he didn't miss even one! We all sang 'Hatikvah,' standing at attention, and then we crashed against each other, out on the dance floor, rocking in convulsive laughter, as the band played the latest heavy metal.

My T-shirt has an inscription on the front of it written in Hebrew letters: 'Gaza was a free-fire zone.' That day comes back to me now as I heat the bottom of the spoon with my lighter. I stir the black island with the plunger of my syringe.

'Seth, get your ass over there and get that kid. We got reports they were firing on us from this house.' I look back at my lieutenant. 'Go inside, goddammit! Use the kid as a shield. They won't fire on a kid.' I do as I am told. The kid's face looks unafraid and determined as I duck-walk him inside the shack. The stink of the place overcomes me, a mixture of burnt cooking oil and human excrement.

My Uzi peeks out from under the kid's arm, like a New Year's bottle rocket, and that's when the kid begins to smile. A huge, swarthy grin scares me. The shots ring out. The kid is hit, falls backward into my arms like a rag doll, like the black dot that melts in the spoon. I fire back, just as the young woman shoots her pistol and screams, falls to the sandy floor, writhing in agony inside her black chador.

I also fall to the floor, wounded in the leg.

I shout out to the lieutenant, who is safe inside his tank, 'You better get your ass in here, Lieutenant. It's a mistake. It's one big mistake in here!' The black island of hope is now melted inside the concave of the spoon. I roll the bead of cotton between my fingertips, place it gingerly on the spoon, and the liquid fills it like Paradise being sucked into a cloud. I dip the tip of the needle into the infused cotton and pull the plunger back—pull the trigger back—pull my soul back into my body, ready for the peace to take over.

I pick up the article published by Amnesty International. I want to re-read the special part as I am injecting. It always gives me a feeling of importance when I turn on. I don't feel like the isolated, dying soldier living with his mother inside an apartment in Tel Aviv. I feel like an important journalist, reporting the facts to the world that will finally listen:

I learned early on that war forms its own culture. The rush of battle is a potent and often lethal addiction, for war is a drug, one I ingested for many years. It is peddled by myth makers—historians, war correspondents, filmmakers, novelists, and the state—all of whom endow it with qualities it often does possess: excitement, exoticism, power, chances to rise above our small stations in life, and a bizarre and fantastic universe that has a grotesque and dark beauty. It dominates culture, distorts memory, corrupts language and infects everything around it, even humor, which becomes preoccupied with the grim perversities of smut and death.

Fundamental questions about the meaning, or meaninglessness, of our place on the planet are laid bare when we watch those around us sink to the lowest depths. War exposes the capacity for evil that lurks just below the surface within all of us. And so it takes little in wartime to turn ordinary men into killers. Most give themselves willingly to the seduction of unlimited power to destroy, and all feel the peer pressure. Few, once in battle, can find the strength to resist.

My mother told me we were once brothers and sisters. Muslims and Jews have the same laws of kashrut: no pork, no shellfish, nothing without fins or scales, no animal that is a predator. Together, they faced the invading Infidels from Christian Europe—the Crusaders—who had the practice of eating the 'body and blood' of their god, Jesus. To Muslims and Jews, Yahweh can never be a flesh-and-blood man. Never shall we eat the flesh of any human or prophet. I knew we had more cultural practices in common with the Muslims than we both had with the Christians. And yet, now the Christians are our allies against the Muslims. How can that be so?

We pack our cultural allies into their refugee camps in Gaza and the West Bank, put up our militant walls and checkpoints all around; we must know all about them, their comings and goings, as if they were an alien race or species—not our brothers and sisters in culture—all because of this land we call our own, and they call their own, and all of our leaders exploit the differences to acquire power and wealth over the other. It is so clear to me now. Exploitation and greed are at the crux of our problems— on both sides—and now the mediator must move in to fill the bottomless crevasse between them.

I am the new Messiah! This is how it's going to be, from this day forward! We shall share collectively what we have. We shall return to the barter system—no more tricky investments based on complicated algorithms that only the rich can comprehend—a simple exchange of goods and services to maintain a healthy and mediated lifestyle. No, and it is not communism.

I say unto you, we are all human beings, and our brains have become our worst enemies! The brain seeks to divide us, to make us puppets to these masters who would use us for their profit, to make us like dreamers after their dreams, not our own. And so it shall be, I am the alien prophet, from another planet, a planet where peace and brotherhood reigns supreme over all. If you do not share, if you do not hold each other in utmost regard, then I will unleash my infinite power of Judgment upon you! I come from Omshanti, and I will lead you!

I set the filled needle down for a moment and pick up a photo album from another era. As I turn the pages, memories are injected into me like the drug I need to stay alive. My mother holds me in her arms at the same hospital where she now works. I was born on February 24, 1984 in Tel Aviv. I am a Pisces, 'very creative but subject to being too much of a dreamer,' my mother told me. There I am at my Bar Mitzvah, standing tall in my blue prayer shawl and reciting my Torah portion, the part about Job giving up his selfish plea of innocence to God and becoming resigned to the omniscient power of his Maker. There I am standing tall in my IDF uniform, my face sunburned from training in the Negev, my grin so self-assured and brimming with a confidence that has now left me forever. Finally, there I am in the ashram, my mother standing beside me next to Guru Sharma; she stares out at the camera, a Mona Lisa in her nurse's role. We left Omshanti that day and moved back to Israel.

I set the photo album down and pick the needle up again. I stare at it. I shall go forth and inject this into all Mankind so they can at last be at peace with themselves! It is the only peace I know, and it will be the only peace they will ever know. There is no peace greater than the peace of the poppy! Oh, noble flower, blooming in the desert, I share your grace with the multitudes. Like the Prophet Jesus, I will make many fishes out of one fish, many loaves out of one loaf, and many injections out of this one! May this be the one to give me the power—the eternal power to control my destiny!

The needle goes inside the crook of my arm, laid out along that red river Styx, and the smile creeps into my face, the smile of the boy, the smile of the culture of war, and my alien head falls forward to rest on my chest. I hum 'Hatikvah,' and wait for the sun to go down.

Darkness brings a calm I can finally endure, as my mother enters from the hospital, and I will once again hold her by her thin shoulders, she is getting so very thin these days, look into her dark eyes, and ask, 'So Eema? How goes the battle?'

She looks up at me, a sad, knowing face that perhaps had looked up at many other prophets and sons, in many other times and places, neither passing judgment nor unduly praising. She just stares.

I, in my reverie, go over to the CD player on the little antique German table my mother has kept for five generations of Bermans. My father, long ago passing into the night of forgotten dreams, does not hold sway anymore. She is the queen of this home. I am her prince.

I play the music and it invokes in her a time from her youth, when children ran freely inside the kibbutz, the socialist farm, and in Omshanti, the American commune. All were parents to these children; all were responsible for their welfare. There was no selfishness imposed by the outside, capitalist forces of the 'free market.' The children, my mother among them, ran, danced and played their infinite variety of games, going from one new parent to another, never discriminating, never questioning their love, never feeling ashamed or fearful that there would come a time when there might be no parent to guard them. The song was a folk song from the kibbutzim, and I caught my mother up in my arms, and we danced as if time stood still, as if there were no more wars for land, for pride, for religion, or even for God. There was only the completed circle of love, alienated from the times to come, frozen in a moment of devotion and joy inside a song of hope.

After our dance, she sits down next to me on the small divan, and I lay my alien head down in her skinny lap and close my eyes. She whispers to me, as I try to sleep, and the words encircle my mind like another kind of drug.

SERENE

'This crisis will pass if you can just understand that you are free without their pressures, without their intoxicants to blind you. The tumor on your brain also contains the light of new beginnings. Ganesha, the elephant-headed god. Don't be afraid, my son. The light of the Zohar, the Ein Sof, is in you. The Secret Garden, in worlds of light hidden . . . its splendor sends forth to the ends of Creation, in the fullness of glory and is revealed in its beauty to the eyes made seeing—the Garden of Eden.'

"Seth? Do you remember me? I was chosen to be the Omshanti bride of passion on the day you told me my parents had died. You ran up to me. Remember? You were just a boy then." My voice came out in gasps. I kept thinking about how the Guru always said there were no coincidences in one's life. Everything happens for a reason, and it is up to me to determine what the reason is.

"Rachel. Yes! Did they ever tell you about why your parents died?" Seth Berman could have been a prophet from the Bible. His words had that kind of effect on me.

"No. Guru Sharma just told me they died working on a secret project, and he said Omshanti would support me for the rest of my life if I wanted it."

"I'm sorry to have to be the one to tell you, but after you were sent away to school, the story came out about how your parents had committed suicide. Somebody had caught them trafficking young boys and girls into the world sex tourism trade. You know, we got a lot of homeless then to get votes, and there were a lot of kids who had no parents. They were there without identification, without a family address, and so I guess your folks saw a chance to make some extra cash. When the Bhagwan found out, I guess they couldn't stand the shame."

I was crushed. All these years, as I studied and improved my mind to become a doctor, my support group had been keeping this dark truth from me! However, I also knew there was a faction within Omshanti that hated the Guru and wanted to bring him and his followers down. Maybe Seth was one of these disgruntled members. He sounded as if he believed he had taken Sharma's place as a redeemer of the planet.

"Why did you leave the group?" I asked.

"When we heard about you getting paid tuition to go to college outside Omshanti, many of us tried to petition Bhagwan to do the same for us. He refused. That's when my mother told him she had enough. She was going to take me back to Israel where I could prosper among our own people. We didn't know there would be all these terrorist intifadas and the Gaza invasions. And then, when they found my brain tumor."

Seth looked down at his lap. The tears were streaming, and I realized I would need more proof to find out whether he was telling me the truth about how my parents had died. His brain tumor could be confusing his memories, and he and his mother might have believed rumors from the faction that hated the Guru and what he stood for. I needed to do some more investigating to see who was being honest with me. As it stood, everyone could be lying to me, including the Israeli government.

What was the implication of seeing a former member of Omshanti in Israel? Not only was he a former member, he was also the one member who had seen my parents' bodies being taken from the commune on that fateful day. I thought I could perhaps put Seth Berman behind me after that day of counselling. He was obviously going to die, and all I could do was keep in touch with his decline and visit him in the hospital. This would not be the case.

Exactly three days after our therapy session, I received a phone call from a woman who said her name was Judith. I was in my office in the hotel interviewing another PTSD patient. "You talked to my son, Seth, last week. We were members of Omshanti."

"Oh, yes! Mrs. Berman. It's so nice to hear from you. I was going to call you to stay on track with your son's progress. How is he?"

"He's been murdered." Her voice was shallow, as if all the tears had already been shed, and I was getting the last bit of sanity from her brain.

"Murdered? How do you know?"

"Whoever killed him sent me an email message while I was working at the hospital. The message told me my son was sacrificed because he was a blasphemer of Maithuna, which is the only hope for mankind's salvation. But it was when and how he was killed that makes this event so mysterious. The authorities said Seth had his throat slit following his ejaculation. Traces of his sperm were on his body and on the bed sheet inside our apartment. His forehead was also inscribed with a black Star of David which had a single red line running through it, like on a road sign. All they've come up with is that Maithuna means one of the positions of lovemaking in the Tantric practice of sacred sex. There was no other physical evidence at the scene. The police believe somebody may have brought him to orgasm just before he or she cut his throat. Obviously, they are looking at this as a hate crime of some sort."

"Of course! What a tragic event for you to have to deal with. Please come to see me if you need some counseling. We have so much history together with Omshanti. In fact, I am wondering if somebody from our group in California might be a possible suspect. You remember, I'm sure, how there were fanatical factions inside the commune that wanted anybody who went against Guru Sharma dead. He helped me get through school, so I owe him something, but there were other members that would threaten the lives of those who spoke ill of him--even if they were members of Omshanti."

I guess I was telling her the wrong thing, because she hung up on me, and I never heard from her again. I still wanted to investigate on my own into this murder as it seemed to implicate those of us from Omshanti who had come to Israel. In fact, as I researched the symbol for the Star of David on the Internet, I saw that some fringe groups saw a way to implicate the usual anti-Semitic rhetoric into this hexagram:

The hexagram, popularly known as the Jewish 'Star of David' or 'Seal of Solomon,' is actually an ancient pagan sex & fertility symbol! The upward triangle is a penis, penetrating the downward triangle of the vulva. Shockingly, the hexagram was unknown to ancient Jews! Jesus never saw it, nor Kings David or Solomon! Even more shockingly, the hexagram is also used by New Agers, conspiracists, witches, and even Satanists!

Guru

Guru Sharma had problems with the Jews who entered Omshanti. Many of them he just let go because they see religion as more of a culture than as a way to escape the repression of governmental regulations. Rachel Edelstein and her parents, Sid and Rose, came to Omshanti because they had no family. They were not Orthodox Jews, so the Guru's teachings did not conflict too much with their Judaic belief system. Omshanti views on accepting science as a way to improve our lot on Earth were especially acceptable to them, as they were both computer science and robotics engineers. Sharma was beginning to increase funding for his laboratory, so they were able to begin work right away on the new Serene project under Dr. Joshua Lawrence.

When Rachel's parents died, he knew he would have a problem on his hands. During their lovemaking in the passion bridal chamber, the girl was in some kind of self-induced trance, and she began talking about being on Masada Mountain in Israel. When he entered her, she did not move a muscle. Instead, her eyes were fixed on the Ganesha statue, and he was never able to get any kind of reaction from her, even with the most heated thrusts of his pelvis. Most girls performed admirably, although some cried, but they told him later they were tears of joy at being a chosen one. Rachel simply looked down at herself bleeding and called for a handmaid to clean her off.

Now she is in Israel, and he realizes she doesn't want to return to Omshanti. She continues to email him, however, and he believes the experiences she has had as a therapist might change her attitude. Many of her patients, she believes, are possibly incurable, damaged beyond all hope. This was the main reason he established his commune. He knew that world governments were forever using their weapons to reap more power and wealth, and they left the people lonely and destitute.

Even in their own peaceful ashram, Omshantians were called worshippers of Satan and sex perverts by the strangers outside. Guru hated to establish the armed guards, but when his motorcade travels through Omshanti each day, and they have tourists amongst his followers, one of these tourists might just be an assassin bent upon his destruction. The Pope and other religious leaders are experiencing the same dangers, and so, too, has it become part of Omshanti existence.

His followers also need therapy of the kind Rachel can provide. He keeps telling her Omshanti is growing, and the group has not turned its back on modern scientific methods. In fact, he just opened up the Serene Project once again, and it will become a major part of what they will be doing in their science component.

He believes that women—especially if they can be freed of the sexual rivalries that a monogamous culture forces upon them—can become the best administrators and doctors Omshanti can have. Rachel would make a perfect therapist for Omshanti. Every woman he has appointed to a responsible position has performed above and beyond expectations. Each has been honest, trustworthy, and innovative.

Yes, Omshanti has had mishaps, such as the first Serene experiment with Rachel's parents, but the Guru wants to continue building the infrastructure that combines a free spirit with an unencumbered scientific quest. One day, Omshanti will establish the bedrock upon which a new world and even—dare he say it—a galactic convergence will take place!

Joshua

SynGen Group, San Diego, August 2014

Office Memoranda
Subject: Project Serene

I have assembled the required staff and ordered the equipment necessary to begin work on the new tests required for trials with the animals. The stated goals are the same as when initially proposed after observing the Omshanti cult for three years. We want to harness the libido of a human subject through the use of artificial intelligence and a physiological implant that references a predetermined package of researched sexually sensitive stimuli that will enable the controller to send enough endorphins into the brain to establish a reflex conditioned response that overcomes any other outside conditioning, such as being a member of cult for several years.

I would like to begin my project next week. Therefore, it is necessary for me to have my staff assigned for at least six months, and I would also like to keep open requisitions for any more new supplies we might need.

Dr. Joshua Lawrence, Head of Genetic AI, Dept. 6A

That's what he had to write to keep the company sleuths off his back. He even had to lie to his staff to a certain extent because they have no idea that they will be researching far beyond the genetic modification of endorphins to control sexual behavior. He wants to be able to prevent any organization such as Omshanti from using so-called "free love" to control members' allegiances and behaviors. True, sex is one of the strongest instincts in the human species, but he wants the individual to be able to control his or her own drive and not any organization—even if it's SynGen. Sex should never be for sale unless the individual is in complete control of how the intercourse is conducted and to whom these precious favors are extended.

Until he was made aware of Dr. Rachel Edelstein, he thought finding a good subject for his human experiment was going to be most difficult. He needed a person who had been damaged by a sexual trauma but who was also intelligent enough to understand the underlying physical problem that must be resolved first before attempting to cure the trauma. As a member of Omshanti, Rachel was chosen to be one of the sex brides of the cult leader, one Bhagwan Sharma. As he has determined by investigating her history with the group and subsequent education, her personal drive to heal her own psychological injury has led her to become a doctor of psychiatry.

His project needs someone with the intellectual skills to appreciate what the Serene implant can do for her. In addition, since she had been a practicing therapist for the Israeli government, he can also be assured she is the personality type who can follow orders and be aware of the dangers of misusing a powerful device such as Serene.

Of course, the final ingredient is familial, as he was able to ascertain that her parents began a similar exploration into the sex drives of humans when they worked in the laboratory at Omshanti. It's not clear how they died, but he believes it was because the couple decided to use themselves as the first human trial subjects. He believes it is appropriate for Dr. Rachel Edelstein to continue this endeavor in the memory of her

SERENE

parents, and the irony is that it may be possible to use her parents' brains to create androids that will continue Rose and Sid forever into the future.

21

CHAPTER THREE: THE SERENE GENESIS

Joshua

Josh discovered the Omshanti cult as a sixteen-year-old grad student at Caltech in Pasadena. Like most geniuses, he had a prematurely developed intellect, but his social skills were not unlike the stereotypical "Sheldon Cooper" from *The Big Bang Theory*. He found that show quite lacking as to the actual lifestyles of engineers and scientists at Caltech and the Jet Propulsion Laboratory. In reality, they dined at the exclusive Athenaeum on campus, which was where he learned to appreciate fine cuisine. On the TV show, we see these scientists eating takeout in their sparse apartments. In reality, scientists lived in relative luxury, as their six-figure salaries would allow, up in the large homes of La Canada Flintridge. That show, in fact, harkens back to an era when scientists shunned profit-making enterprises and believed their experimentation should be shared amongst the world's best minds in order to improve the environmental and socio-political health of humanity.

Not so. Today, corporate think tanks and Wall Street investment firms harvest most of the great minds trained at the prestigious universities around the world. As a result, America of today is not the representative democracy that *perhaps* was envisioned by the founders, although there are arguments against that actually being the case. America of today is an oligarchy, and as such, corporations want to own genomes and not share them. They want to increase profits to their shareholders and not increase the health and wellbeing of our teeming populace.

As a sixteen-year-old, he was looking for some kind of social institution that could provide sexual gratification to a person who did not want to go through the elaborate and demeaning mating process dictated by the American culture. Why couldn't we just "cut to the chase" and "get it on" as the childlike hippies used to say? Free love still existed, and it was being shared at the Omshanti commune in San Marcos, California. That was all he needed to know.

He made it his sole purpose to investigate this organization and find out if what it was advertising on the Internet was actually true. He could care less about the Hindu mumbo-jumbo. As an Ayn Rand enthusiast and lifelong atheist, he had long ago, by age thirteen, put away the *Bible, Koran, Bhagavad Gita,* and *Dhammacakkappavattana Sutta* in exchange for *Atlas Shrugged* and *Beyond Good and Evil.* Now he wanted to see theory put into practice on a first-person level.

San Marcos wasn't too far from the Caltech campus, so he drove down there on a weekend to attend one of the group's tours of the ashram. He would be able to stay at the hotel right inside Omshanti's ten acres of "organic horticulture, modern science labs, and active meditation temple," but of course all he cared about was information concerning the perhaps more animalistic erotic sharing of body parts.

When he filled out the online questionnaire, the group contacted him, and a honey-voiced female was on the phone to welcome him. She told him that Guru Bhagwan Sharma himself had viewed his application. "As you might be aware, Omshanti is hoping to attract the greatest minds from around the world to join our group. As a result of your qualifications, Mr. Lawrence, we are placing you in our exclusive tour of the ashram. You will be able to visit our science labs and see what kind of equipment we have at your disposal as well our university-level library that is being supplemented daily with digital access to the most advanced engineering and scientific journals in the world."

He almost wanted to shout into the telephone that he could care less about their advanced science and technology. "Just show me the tits and ass!" was what his sixteen-year-old mind was thinking. However, as he knew that kind of invective would isolate him from their collective religious delusion, he kept his desires to himself and said, "Thank you. I am looking forward to the tour."

The genesis of his Serene project, as one might assume by now, began with the tour that day. He still had his journal's notes that he completed at night in their Active Meditation Hotel. You'll have to excuse the rather sophomoric descriptions of the fleshly delights, but he was, after all, a raging hormonal adolescent. Is it no wonder that the Supreme Court had finally judged the teenaged brain so lacking in decision-making abilities that no longer may the states execute such brains for murderous intent? At that age, god help us, we are not able to curtail our lustful urges.

Today we were guided, until lunch, to the horticultural hothouse and the 'futuristic' research laboratory. Four others in my 'exclusive group' were also teenage geniuses from Caltech and UCSD, and one flew all the way out from MIT. As per usual, we did not talk amongst ourselves. Instead, I assumed we each were collecting our cynical thoughts to be later transcribed into journals such as this to be shared with our fellow introverts on our secluded online bulletin boards.

I didn't find much in the way of new research being done by these people wearing the cult's ashram orange (a color most indicative to good fortune in the Hindu culture). The hybridization of vegetables had been perfected long ago by Israeli farmers on kibbutzim and by Japanese using organic hydroponics inside their over 52,000 hectares of greenhouses. If I were to guess which culture makes the best horticulturalists, I would say that the ones that are island nations and are desert nations should be used as the touchstone for the best and most advanced research and development. Indeed. All that we in the U.S. seem to have developed is corn that can sterilize vast fields of non-genetically modified plants. The Omshanti scientists did have a rather unique way of growing spinach on floating beds of water suspended from the ceiling. Other than that, most of their other innovations were copies of basic cross-breeding accomplished the world over.

As for the science lab experiments, again, although the equipment was advanced, the research being conducted that we were allowed to see was mundane. The exception was the genetic sequencing machine they had. Twelve years ago, it cost $1 billion to sequence a single human genome. By next year, using Life Technologies' Ion Proton machine, it will take less than a day and cost $1,000 (not including analysis costs, of course). The Omshanti genetics lab had one of these Ion Proton machines, and this was something even Caltech did not have. The MIT woman said her school had one, but I always take what MIT says with a pound of sodium.

It didn't get interesting until after a lunch of organically grown carrots, peas and non-GMO corn and chickpeas. We were all led by the Guru Bhagwan Sharma in a guided "active meditation" that was unlike any meditation I had ever experienced. My parents, who were once hippie commune members, never exercised this kind of meditation. I had always been instructed that meditation's purpose was to keep the mind clear, relaxed, and inwardly focused. When you meditate, you are fully awake and alert, but your mind is not focused on the external world or on the events taking place around you. Meditation requires an inner state that is still and one-pointed so that the mind becomes silent. When the mind is silent and no longer distracts you, meditation deepens.

Conversely, there was the 'active meditation' of the Omshantians. We began with what I call 'navel gazing,' which is the traditional form of meditation that my parents practiced. However, then the transformation began into the 'active' part. Did I mention this all took place inside the huge 'temple' where every member of the Serene family ate and meditated as a group? Not only was I monkeying along with over 900 orange-clad, underwear-donning idiots, I was also being led into the very sexual frenzy that had provoked my interest in this group from the very beginning, when I saw the short video of several bare-breasted damsels smiling out at me on the web. Each had the necklace with the attached picture of Guru Sharma's bearded and dark face, and those hypnotic brown eyes that drilled holes into you.

All the Guru said was 'Let the demons go!' and boy did we start to demonize. The woman beside me began to scream like I had seen only once before. It was in a documentary on one of those apostolic Christian sects in which members 'spoke in tongues' and began writhing and babbling on the floor like insane inmates. It began to get interesting, however, when Bhagwan said, 'Let the love fill your lotus hearts like an eternal spring of passion!'

The woman beside me took off her orange blouse, and all I could watch was the picture of Guru Sharma as it bounced between her voluptuously bulbous and nippled young breasts. There was no music playing. The music, I assumed, came from within. After most of the congregation was half or fully naked, with penises flailing about like Kundalini snakes and buttocks jiggling like mounds of fleshly honeypots, the Guru finally said, 'Find your heart's desire!'

On cue, the members began bouncing around and staring deeply into the eyes of each other. Male on male, female on female, and of course, the traditional coupling of male and female. It was all happening before my pubescent eyes. What was I doing amid this hurricane of animal desire? Although fully erect beneath my Dockers, I stood at parade rest, my hands behind my back, observing the scene the way Dr. Oppenheimer must have on that day he watched children playing in the streets and said, 'They could solve some of my top problems in physics because they have modes of sensory perception that I lost long ago.' I was at last finding my modes of sensory perception that had disappeared during my years of study and devotion to science. I knew that at sixteen I would finally be able to produce adult research because I had found a wellspring of passion right there in the center of that group of dancing Shivas and Shaktis. The genesis of my Serene research began with a single hypothesis: If I can create an artificially stimulating way to harness the libido of a human being, I could prevent cults like this one from controlling its members for the personal gain and enrichment of the leader. I wanted to return the control of passion back to the individual, and use science to create a device that could physiologically monitor the body's true passion centers and replicate them for the individual to enjoy—even alone—if the brain's need so determines it.

I did not pair off with anyone that day. However, I vowed to allow myself such pleasure once I was able to create the Serene AI device that was forming in my brain like a genetically modified passion seed.

Josh decided to join the Omshanti group at some point after his graduation. He made it his quest to enjoy the world's cuisine during his research to create the Serene device, and he was also going to enjoy the world's sexual practices, one person at a time, until his device became a way for entire societies to free themselves from control by the media or by gurus such as Bhagwan Sharma, and to allow each person to become the completely unrepressed human that was waiting to be born into a new world of the elevated senses.

CHAPTER FOUR: THE RAPE

Tel Aviv, Israel, October 2014

Rachel

The last patient I saw in Israel was Corporal Sarah Landon, 28, who had been raped by her commanding officer while they were raiding suspected terrorist homes inside Gaza. Of course, she wasn't the only female I treated for sexual trauma from rape. Even though the IDF had far fewer such reported rape incidents than we did in the U.S., there was still an average of one in eight female soldiers who said they had been sexually harassed by their superior officers. The fact that most rapes go unreported in the military happens because the military tries its own felons, and the majority of the military court martial proceedings are conducted and led by men. If you were a woman who had been raped, would you believe you would get a fair prosecution of the accused?

Therefore, we military psychiatrists and counselors were the ones who had to treat the collateral damage from this kind of patriarchal chauvinism that exists in the military. However, once again, it was not just the heinous act of rape that made Corporal Landon's story so important in my arriving at the decision to resign my commission in the Israeli Defense Forces. Once again, let me recreate that day for you. As I am no longer directly affiliated with the Israeli Government, the doctor/patient confidentiality law does not apply.

Sarah was a short woman with kinky black hair that she swept into a neat bun. As a Spanish or Sephardic Jew, her face was darker than the Russians and yet she was still lighter complexioned than the Yemenites or, of course, the black Ethiopian Jews who joined the military. Her color had nothing to do with what happened to her, but it was certainly her trust in her commanding officer that had caused the incident to happen. Once again, the coincidental fact that she had once been a member of our tiny Omshanti group in San Marcos, California, was ultimately the major factor in my decision to resign. In Israel, she had joined the Nahal Infantry

Brigade's 931 battalion, which had fought some of the most intense, complex battles during Operation Protective Edge.

After I put Sarah under, she stared off into space and related the following story to me:

We were doing night raids into the poor sections of Gaza. Hamas would often hide their munitions for rocket launchers inside these tiny apartments, so we had to search them out with dogs and metal detectors. We kept our night vision goggles on, so I guess we looked like invaders from another planet.

My commanding officer was Lieutenant Avi Berkowitz. I guess my mistake came when I told him how I had once belonged to a cult in California that chose me to be a bride of passion. We were out in the personnel carrier talking about how ISIS and other terrorist groups in Africa were using women as sex slaves. The others in our platoon listened. They didn't say a word. But the lieutenant sounded quite sympathetic to these women and their plight, and he condemned the unholy methods of these fanatical Muslims.

I thought, why not tell him about my experience with Guru Sharma? So, I told the lieutenant that when I was a young girl I lived on a religious fanatic's commune, and he chose one girl each year to fuck inside his private bedroom, and he called us the brides of passion. He told us he needed to make it with a virgin because it was the only way he could bring the Andromeda Galaxy closer to our Milky Way. You see, the Guru said he was originally from a planet in the Andromeda Galaxy and that we would one day become mingled together and practice the same traditions for the peaceful sharing of love and freedom. Oh, and by the way, you need to fuck me to make it happen! I was only thirteen years old, for heaven's sake!

Again. Nobody in our unit said a word. I was the only female, so I guess they were just fantasizing or some other such thing.

I expected him to show compassion again at that point. For me. Yes, I'll admit, he was kind of cute, so a close hug would not have been out of place. However, when he told me he wanted to talk to me in private when we returned to the base, I should have known something wasn't right. Officers and enlisted are not supposed to fraternize, but stupid bitch that I was, I went with him to his civilian apartment off-base in Tel Aviv.

At first, he handed me a glass of wine and sounded very sympathetic. He told me how courageous I was to volunteer for front-line duty, and he also said that to be a military leader I must learn that orders are meant to be followed. He told me he could give me a field advancement, and I could be a sergeant the next day. He then took his cock out of his trousers and gave me a direct order to suck him off.

Okay, I'll admit, I wanted to make more money, and sucking him off was far from the free love I had experienced at Omshanti, so I did it. But, when I started going down on him, he grabbed my hair, and forced me backward toward the bed. He was a big guy—about six feet four, 230 pounds—so I didn't try to fight him off. In fact, I thought if I could get hold of a morning after pill I would be able to live with it. But I had vowed once I left the commune to never again allow somebody to make love with me unless he wanted to be married to me. So, I refused. And he slapped me. When I wouldn't take off my fatigues, he punched me—hard.

Afterward, I took my pill, but then I began to hate being in the same room or vehicle with him. He was an ever-present reminder of how I had been violated. I never got the advancement, either. In fact, I began to hear chuckles from the other men in the platoon. They started calling me 'bride of passion.' I knew it would just be a matter of time before I would be walking alone somewhere and one or more of these guys would jump me.

"So, what did you do?" I couldn't help asking. I was so transfixed by her story that I was having a difficult time concentrating on my job as her counselor. My own mind was flashing back to the day I had been violated inside that same bridal chamber of horrors. The noxious smell of the man's body odor mixed with the perfumed incenses of that rapist's torture room. My body revolted at his touch, but at least I was not struck or punched. This poor woman had been raped, and then she became the fantasy of other would-be rapists. My experience, no matter how much it had affected my attitude toward sex, was not nearly as traumatic as Sarah's had been. I guess the drug and hypnosis gave her the extra courage she needed. She told me the horrendous truth.

I heard that Hamas was using civilian neighborhoods to build underground tunnels to shuttle rockets closer to the neighborhoods in Israel. They also treated the homes as military locations, and there would often be booby-trapped explosives inside waiting for us. I decided to use my own form of trap on my platoon.

One night we were on a mission going house-to-house, and I told the guys I wanted to go into the house first. Once inside, I stripped off my fatigue top, then my sports bra. I radioed my platoon that it was safe to enter. When they came inside the house and saw me standing in the back bedroom with my breasts heaving and a smile on my face, they began to disrobe almost in unison. They actually believed in the whore myth they had created for me in their lustful imaginations. When they were naked, I told them I would not party with them unless they wore protection. Only the lieutenant had a condom, so I told them to wait while I went back outside to the personnel carrier. I told them I had more condoms in my backpack inside the APC.

I had done my research inside the Tel Aviv library. Practical Bomb Scene Investigation, second edition, gave me the knowledge, and I obtained the tools. I created an improvised device worthy of Hamas, and guess who got blamed when I detonated the explosives that were hidden inside that bedroom? My watch contained the transmitter device that actually coded the signal that would be decoded on the receiver affixed to my bomb inside the bedroom. I knew that because there were all kinds of powerful signals being transmitted in that war-torn neighborhood I would need the specialized coding to set off my improvised explosive device without having it accidentally detonated by another signal.

When I heard the explosion inside the house, I actually felt as if the bomb had lifted my spirit out of my body and into the night air. When the medics came for me, I was all alone inside the APC. When headquarters told me my entire platoon had been killed by the Hamas booby-trap, I broke down, and they, of course, gave me a medical discharge.

Sarah was able to be discharged, but two days after her meeting with me, the IDF military police paid me a personal visit at my office in Tel Aviv. It seems the same ritualistic murder had taken place, complete with the black Star of David with a line through it drawn upon her forehead, but this time it was a female member of our military who was the victim. Sarah had been found with her throat slashed, and the tall inspector Captain named Levin, with a bushy black mustache, informed me that the cut was done in the kosher *shechitah* method. It must have been a *chalif* knife because this kind of slaughtering knife can have no nicks or abrasions—of even a hair's width—so it can cut the esophagus, trachea, carotid arteries, and jugular veins in one quick incision with no pain. The blood from her body was also drained completely, but there was no sperm present as was the case with Seth Berman. If she died after orgasm, it must have been reached through self-stimulation or from a foreign object like a dildo.

I was questioned about my job and my former life on the Omshanti commune. I guess the Israeli Government also found it too coincidental that we all came from the same strange cult in California. They assured me they would be in touch, but since I had an iron-clad alibi for where I had been during both of these murders (I was treating patients), they could not keep me from doing what I wanted to do.

Following this second murder, I decided to leave the IDF forever. I wanted to go home to America and become a family practitioner. Whether I would return to Omshanti or not was not on my plate at that moment. I did know that if I stayed in the IDF I would, most likely, become the next victim. Now I had to uncover the truth about these murders and if they were somehow related to my parents' deaths. If I got out of the military, maybe the killer would not follow me back to America.

I also began to research part of my heritage that had been forbidden to me. The Kabbalah is the ancient practice of understanding how the world came to be and how there was still a divine presence within existence that can be reached through the practice of certain principles.

I found a website at Temple Emanuel where Rabbi Miriam Price taught a monthly study group of Kabbalah enthusiasts. When I read the following explanation by her, I decided to join this group when I returned home:

We must see that the ego self creates a false perception of Heaven in the here-and-now based on its selfish perception of everything. We study Kabbalah to learn there is no self or I. There is only the Ein Sof, the ultimate light that unites all reality. Once this is achieved inside of you, the union of the spirit will come to pass.

However, the first person I wanted to connect with was a psychiatrist who was recommended to me by the IDF, believe it or not. They said he specialized in treating officers and more educated clientele. As luck would have it, he was also a member of Rabbi Price's Kabbalah study group in San Diego. I first met him that night when I attended the group.

The study of the Kabbalah was the closest to mysticism in Jewish culture. My parents never practiced any organized religion, as they were basically New Age hedonists, but I was always attracted to the study of all things that have a spiritual or mystical quality. I suppose it helps balance the use of my mind as a psychiatrist, which requires a logical, deductive approach to the cases I work on.

I attended a study group at the Kabbalah Centre. We had to move every month to a different location, as our discipline was not considered in the mainstream of Judaic thought. That day we were at a Baptist Church near San Diego State University. Rabbi Price took a collection each session so we could pay for the place we rented.

Rabbi Miriam Price was a Reform Jew who donated her time to teach us spiritual seekers about how God can be reached on the physical plane of existence by meditation and by mystical practices that concentrate on the Ten Sefirot, which God used to send forces of compassion and severe justice into His Creation. Our teacher made it clear to us the first night that we wouldn't be studying Kabbalah to increase our sex drive, to get rich and famous, or to put curses on our enemies. She always pointed to the Tiferet element on her cardboard chart of the "Big Ten."

Rabbi Price was in her early forties, with reddish-brown hair that was long, and she always looked directly at you, as if you were filled with the divine light. She had a perpetually amused demeanor, which made her quite attractive. She wore plain grey suits with white blouses, which was a kind of statement against promoting the ego.

"We need to learn how to balance our male and female aspects—the nine other elements—so we can experience the *Shekhinah, Malkhut.*" The *Shekhinah* was the feminine presence of God in this world, and Rabbi Price loved talking about that!

That night, the good rabbi was lecturing about how the responsibility for change is always placed on us. As she spoke, I kept looking at the Christian icons all around the church. The white cross, the colorful painting of the blond-haired, blue-eyed Jew, Jesus, and the many copies of the *New Testament* lying around. To us Jews, this so-called "new" testament might as well be a fairytale by the Brothers Grimm. The only book we knew was the Hebrew Scriptures. It was both our history and our mythology. The *Kabbalah*, on the other hand, was our Jewish fairytale.

"We have free will to choose evil or good, so the ten emanations are merely symbolic representations we can study to make wise choices," Price said.

I was poked in the arm by a new guy sitting next to me. He was smiling, and I liked his looks. He didn't have the horny gaze that I got from all the other straight men in the study group. He whispered to me, "Of course, all religions should be taken on a symbolic level. These symbols are then used according to how each symbol appears to the individual."

I didn't know exactly what he was talking about, but when he approached me during the break with his Styrofoam cup of coffee and cookie, I thought I'd follow up on his point. I was not in the market for romance, but I liked this guy's demeanor. He was also athletically built, tall, dark, and he had a Michael Douglas smile.

"Why did you make that comment about symbols?" I asked him, nibbling on my cookie.

"I'm a Jungian psychoanalyst. My name's Jacob Stein. Dr. Jung broke from Freud and began interpreting dreams on a much more symbolically extreme level. For example, poets use symbols that resonate with any person—no matter his or her ethnicity—so we can experience deeper levels of meaning on a mythical level. That's why *Kabbalah* interests me. I study symbols all the time in my work."

"Oh yeah? Maybe you can help me. I keep having this one dream about Masada, and in it I am one of the Jews who has to choose whether or not to commit suicide or be captured by the Romans and forced to worship their false gods. Why do you think I would keep dreaming this?"

"I really can't say here. Maybe you can drop by my office at the UCSD Medical Center. I can do a consult without any social distractions. What's your line of work?"

"Sorry. I'm a psychiatrist. Rachel Edelstein. Believe it or not, the IDF recommended that I look you up when I got back to the States. I wish I could just get Rabbi Price to build me a golem mud man to confront all the perverts I have to counsel in my practice. Maybe my nightmares would disappear. Hey, but psychoanalysis is good too, right? You have a card?"

Dr. Dreamboat handed me his card, and we returned to our pews for another round of "Name That Sefirot." The way he kept looking over at me and smiling during the rest of Price's lecture gave me a few goosebumps. Was I interested in more than getting my dreams interpreted? How much could I reveal to a man— even if he was a doctor of psychiatry?

I didn't tell him about the murders until our third session during the three weeks at his office in Hillcrest. All I told him was about my traumatic experience as a bride of passion and the fact that I couldn't get intimately close to any male—my gender of choice. He was, of course, a Jungian psychoanalyst, so he was all up on dream symbols and interpretations, but after I told him about the murders, he suddenly became more interested in my physical safety. In fact, after our third hour together, he invited me to his home in the La Jolla Hills, and I reluctantly accepted. I told him how I had to be on medication to go out-of-doors, and he said he would "send his man around to pick me up."

Meeting Jacob

La Jolla, California, present day

I could see how much more profitable it was treating wealthy mental cases than treating poor ones. Dr. Jacob Stein's four-bedroom, three-bath home overlooked La Jolla Cove, some of the most valued property in the United States. My little Golf had its problems circumnavigating the corner on the steep incline, but I was able to park it and turn the wheels away from the curb in front of his house. I was not going into the driveway because I had enough rumors going on in the media about me after a report got out about my uncovering the murders in Israel.

As I walked up the driveway leading to his front door, I looked down to the right and saw the cove below. This was where the seal-loving environmentalists were constantly facing off with the tourist-loving business owners as to whether the barking mammals should be allowed to sunbathe on the cove's sandy beach. It might as well be the Israelis versus the Palestinians. Nobody's won yet, but the seals keep losing.

I was wearing some skinny jeans and a UCSD hoodie. Jacob texted me that it was going to be an informal dinner, so I knew it wasn't prom night.

Jacob's house was built right into the cliff, just the way architect Frank Lloyd Wright did with some of the homes he designed. There was a koi pond on the right as I walked through the front door, and a Jewish psychiatrist who greeted me in the foyer wearing a Japanese turquoise kimono with long gray sleeves. Oh, wait. It was Jacob.

The interior of the place was a mixture of Japanese samurai and California surfer, with hanging paper lanterns and swords, intricate bonsai plants on different tables around the living room, a simple tangerine-colored couch, Asian rug and coffee table, and an interesting antique reddish-brown chest against the wall next to the fireplace. The posters on the walls featured all the world's great surfing spots.

I sat down on the couch. With no words, Jacob walked over to the chest and unlocked it with a key he extracted from his kimono. He reached down into one of the drawers and lifted something metal out of it. He brought what I could see was a handgun over with him to the couch, and he sat down next to me. The Beach Boys were singing over the DVD stereo, "Help me, Rhonda."

"This is a Glock 19, which is basically the compact version of the nine. This is the Generation 4 that is small enough to fit into a woman's hand, and it has a dual recoil spring system that acts to reduce the amount of recoil felt by the shooter. It accepts 10, 15, 17 and 33-round magazines, giving you plenty of ammunition to deal with a threat."

I took a deep breath. "I was brought up believing that if you had enough love in your heart, you wouldn't need a weapon."

"I agree. However, when other people—like ISIS—want to twist love into expressions of hate, then it becomes a matter of self-preservation. I certainly wish we lived in a world where aggression wasn't seen as the way to remedy problems of all kinds. I've spent most of my life working against that kind of thinking."

"Death worship. Isn't that what you said Freud called it?" I was trying to use his psychology on him.

"I was once a pacifist. But one day a patient of mine, who turned out to be paranoid schizophrenic, changed my thinking. In this patient's dreams, he was being pursued by the government, and he told me while conscious that he had been secretly given a brain implant when he was under surgery for his appendix. Now his pursuers could follow his daily activity. I tried treating him with antidepressants, but one day he came in, and I could see he was extremely agitated. Finally, in a fit of emotional paranoia, he pulled out a handgun and pointed it at me."

"My god! What happened?"

"I honestly thought he was going to kill me, but at the last moment, he turned the gun's muzzle back and thrust it under his jaw. When he pulled the trigger, the bullet easily passed through his head to his brain stem causing instant death. I knew then that unless I had a way to protect myself, I could become one of the over 6,000 handgun deaths each year."

"I can see your argument. Let me hold it. I've never even held a gun before." I took the gun from him, and he was right, it did fit easily into my hand. It was also very lightweight. I turned it over and felt the embossed metal on the handle. "So it won't slip out of my hand, right?"

"Right. You know, as a psychiatrist, I am only obligated to report those patients who make direct threats against a specifically named person or persons. The patient who drew the gun on me, however, never threatened anybody specifically, but he was still a danger to himself and others. I think we need to change that law. The shooter at Virginia Tech didn't threaten anybody specifically, either. But he still gunned down 32 of his fellow students. These people shouldn't be allowed anywhere near a gun."

"I see the same kind of thing in my practice. The legal system is weighted too much in favor of protecting the defendant against the state. Nobody wants to defend the victim's rights. You'd be surprised to hear how many of these victims and their families take the law into their own hands. Now, with these plastic guns that are created with 3D printers, they can come into court during sentencing and blow away the person they believe should have been given the death penalty."

"I don't want you to become a victim, so take this gun. It's like rock, paper, scissors. Gun beats knife. We'll get the paperwork done, and then I'll take you over to Ruffin Road to a shooting range. You need to learn how to shoot. Are you ready to eat?"

I was hungry, and I handed the pistol back to Jacob. "You sure you don't want to go hunt for our dinner, Sensei?"

Jacob stood up and stretched. "No, we have some very good sushi and a bit of sake. Did you know that the Japanese don't allow handguns or rifles? In fact, even off-duty police officers are banned from carrying guns. You can buy a shotgun or an air rifle, but it's not easy. First, you have to take a class and a written exam. Then there's a skill test at a shooting range. Next is a drug test. Then a mental evaluation. Assuming you pass all those tests, you file with the police, who then run a background check. No wonder Japan has one of the lowest gun ownership rates in the world."

"But, does it work?" I asked, walking into the dining room where we were going to sit in pillows on the floor.

"For example, in 2008, the U.S. had 12,000 gun-related murders. Japan had 11. More than double that number were killed in the massacre in Newtown, Connecticut. One kid with some guns slaughtered all those children. When it comes to guns, I like Japan's policies. Sadly, we don't have them, so we need to protect ourselves."

After dinner, I was buzzing a bit from the wine, and when Jacob put his moves on me, I didn't resist. He pressed his lips against my throat, and I might have actually cooed like a pigeon. My nipples rose to meet his palms, which were gently massaging my breasts, but I began to have a sensation of growing doom as he walked over to the night table and turned off the lamp. Behind Jacob's naked form were other forms—other men standing and waiting their turn. They followed closely behind him as he slid under the sheets. I could hear them murmuring and coughing, and I could see each of their erections waiting for me to appease it.

My lips began to purse as I felt Jacob's penis against my body, but when I thought about sucking him off, the sounds of the other men became louder, and their bodies pressed closer to the bed in the darkness. I would never finish them all. It was impossible. I knew they couldn't be real, but there they were, and my hallucination had become a reality. I slid out of the bed, breathing heavily, and stood at the side. I was shivering and sweating at the same time.

"I can't do it. I'm sorry, but I can't. You're my doctor, and I have to leave," I told Jacob. I certainly didn't want to tell him about what I was experiencing, but the fear was real, and I knew I had to get out of there.

He turned on the lamp. "All right, Rachel. Don't worry. It's my fault. I let my own desire get the best of this situation. Please come with me to the shooting range, and I will see you next week for your regular session."

I decided to take him up on the training. All we got in the IDF was rifle training and some martial arts, so I knew I would benefit from having a weapon on my person, especially after what had happened in Israel.

I decided to keep my relationship with Dr. Stein at the level of exploring the Kabbalah and not exploring my sexual problems. He was a very intelligent and attractive man, but he overstepped his boundary when he agreed to be my bed partner—even if I was the one who had initiated it.

CHAPTER FIVE: SCIENTIFIC GROWTH

Guru

San Marcos, San Diego County California, present day

"I'm sorry about these security measures, but our enterprise must maintain secrecy from those powers we were talking about in the car. Just as you helped us stop the Bride of Passion ceremony, the authorities would shut us down in a heartbeat if they knew about our research," Bhagwan Sharma says, guiding Rachel down a pathway leading to a tall front gate that has warning signs about being private property and razor wire strung along the top. She has finally agreed to visit Omshanti now that she is back in San Diego. He tells her he has a surprise awaiting her and that she will find Omshanti's new scientific efforts, under the direction of Dr. Joshua Lawrence, to be on the order of revolutionary progress.

When they reach the front door, he takes out a black bracelet and wraps it around her right wrist.

"Every person who works here has one of these. It's a sensor that functions the same way as a GPS in a cell phone. However, it's on a very secure network meant for only those affiliated with our organization. Not only can we see where people are at any moment, we can also signal them for meetings and for lunch and other break time activities."

"I completely understand," she says.

"The black plastic wrist band isn't the most fashionable accoutrement one could wear, but the purpose is reasonable, I trust," he tells her.

"You're not the only organization that has enemies," Rachel says, taking in all the greenery that fills the quad they are walking toward. There are many different gardens that grow a variety of vegetables and fruits that are in the ground, on the trees and on the vines that meander through wooden trellises.

"These grounds take up about one-half mile of space, and on the perimeter are the dozens of laboratories, meeting rooms and lecture halls we use for research, planning and education," Guru says.

"When I was working as a psychiatrist for the IDF, two of my patients were murdered. They were both former members of Omshanti. One was Seth Berman and the other was Sarah Landon. We believe the killer had some kind of anti-Semitic agenda because of the way the bodies were desecrated. That Glock you confiscated from me is for my protection in case I might be next on the killer's list." Rachel's brown eyes are glistening with emotion.

As they walk onto the campus, he decides to tell her about how he recruited Joshua Lawrence. It has a lot to do with her past history, with what she believed to be the sexual abuse at his hands, and since she is going to be facing her past, he wants her to know the main reason why he wishes for her to become part of the commune again.

"I'll have my people look over your mobile devices and ensure they will be secure. If this murderer is or was a member of my group, then you need to be safe from any hacker who wants to follow your movements. You can also be certain our goals are to improve the collective ability of science and technology and to serve the people and not to persecute them. If there's a killer in our midst, we want to find him right away." He opens a door to one of the laboratories, and they enter.

Inside this lab are about five different exhibits of machines, medical equipment, and prosthetics, some of which are connected to computers and others standing alone. He walks over to one of the men who is an amputee and puts his hand on the man's shoulder. "Pablo, could you show our guest how you can use your arm? Please note that Pablo has had surgery to implant the necessary advanced technology in electrode arrays and data processing to allow him to send signals from his brain to the arm."

Pablo is able to grasp a pencil that is on the tray, and he begins to write on a paper pad. The act of writing is flawlessly smooth. From the elbow joint down to each finger and thumb, each part of the arm reacts to exactly what is being sent from Pablo's brain.

He then walks over to the next two lab workers, one woman and one man, who are standing next to a man who is seated in a chair. The woman picks up a cord and plugs it into a computer. "Mr. Waldon is an epileptic. I am now going to artificially trigger a grand mal seizure in his brain by attaching this contact to his brain with this helmet. Please note how quickly the implanted sensor discovers this seizure and then sends the electronic signal from the circuit implant to stop the seizure instantly."

She attaches the helmet to Waldon's head, and he immediately begins to convulse. His shoulders shake, his eyes roll back inside their sockets, but then, after about five seconds, the jerking stops, and he is completely normal, sitting still and smiling back at us.

"We also have this implant for alcoholics, addicts and obsessive compulsive types. Whenever the urge to obsess overcomes them, they receive a signal to abstain," says the other technician.

"We have plans to do implants for all types of neurological problems including Parkinsonism symptoms, Alzheimer's, and even Lewy Body Dementia," he says, moving down to the next exhibit.

"This is wonderful!" Rachel is visibly impressed. "You'll be able to help so many people with these devices."

They observe several more of these exhibits, which are obviously set up for her benefit, but they are quite fascinating and help to show her how she would be serving an

SERENE

organization that knows what it is doing. He points out nanorobot cameras that are microscopic in size. He explains how these are injected into the body to replace the very uncomfortable colonoscopy procedure that is being used presently in most hospitals. There are also a variety of new kinds of flying drones, but none is the militant kind. One drone can fly like a bat, using radar sensors to navigate around any obstacles.

"These drones will not hinder commercial or other aircraft the way the current drones are doing. These two large drones can carry shipments of up to a ton without any problem."

The sun is going down and it is streaming through the transom in the roof onto the metallic surfaces of robots as they do their work in the hothouse gardens. The light sparkles and careens off the moving parts, which are synchronous and fluid, tending to each branch, vine, fruit and vegetable with the utmost precision and care. He has never seen any human do work with that much micromanaged organization.

"Our robots are programmed with all the farming methods devised throughout history so that our produce can survive in the worst climates and with the best harvesting processes available." He walks over to one of these robots, which stands about three feet high and looks human in shape, but they all sound like the whirring electronic energy they are powered by. "We're also developing robots that can care for infants and the elderly. These are tasks that can best regulate the health and wellbeing of our species. Not that their caretaking will be limited to humans. Animal husbandry will also be within their expertise."

When the sensor on Rachel's wrist begins to speak to her, she jumps.

Greetings, Rachel. We will be convening in the dining hall for lunch. Please follow the laser light to your destination.

She looks down at the floor and a glowing white light appears. It is in the shape of a ball. It bounces, and she follows it all the way into the dining hall. He follows her.

The large dining hall is expertly organized. The same robots that had worked as gardeners are now serving the garden's delights to the humans seated at round tables all around the room. There are nice white tablecloths and linen napkins, and the silverware is arranged in the European setting. The odor of the vegan fare permeates the large hall with delicious aromas.

"Our studies have shown that the vegan lifestyle is the healthiest for humans, as long as it is supplemented with enough protein. We know that a lot of the greenhouse gasses come from the millions of cattle being raised to satiate the fast-food chains, so we have eliminated that problem." He guides Rachel over to a special round table in the front of the room. It has a large "reserved" sign in the center, and when she sees who is sitting around it, she screams.

Her shock is palpable, so Guru Sharma decides to speak first.

"No, these life-like robots are not your parents, Rachel. However, we have gone to great lengths to create them from videos and photographs of Sid and Rose. What makes these robots ingenious is the way Dr. Lawrence was able to use their digital brain scans to create the central processing units that run the robotic mechanics."

"Oh, yes! Your mother and I have worked here for seventeen years, and we are completely enthusiastic about what we've accomplished," Sid speaks to Rachel.

"Guru Sharma tells us you study Kabbalah now. What have you learned?" her mother says.

"They look so real! May I touch one?" He nods to her, and Rachel walks gingerly over to her mother and touches her face. "It's just like skin," she says.

"It is. We can grow genetically reproduced human skin that we use on these robots," he tells her.

"I think what you're doing here is amazing. You also said all of these inventions will be used to directly help people wherever they live," Rachel says.

"This new technology is going to connect the world and protect it from harm," says Sid, the robot father. "Rachel, I know why you've come. You can rest assured that your mother and I have been converted from the selfishness we lived in our youth. The truth is, each of us is a different person every second we live, and there is always the possibility to change for the better. We hope we can make it up to you and give you what you always needed. We have the time to make it all up to you now, darling. Our self-perpetuating evolution makes this possible."

After they finish lunch, Guru walks with Rachel and her robot parents back to their living quarters. He can tell by how animated she is with these androids that he will probably be able to convince her to come back to the commune. He knows he still needs to explain himself concerning the sexual initiation when she was a girl, but this can be handled in the near future. The world needs Omshanti science and its spiritual rejuvenation right now. This makes any personal traumas one might experience much less important in the grand scheme of things.

Rachel

I have to take an extra dose of thiopental to travel up to San Marcos with Guru Sharma. Just his being in the same car, his fifth new Rolls, makes my skin crawl with memories of that day inside his rape chamber. In fact, I don't really know why I'm doing this except that I need to visit this place again to be able to connect my psyche with the memories that caused my neurotic fractures.

The first thing out of his mouth is that Omshanti stopped the Bride of Passion ritual immediately after I left the commune. He tells me the payments for my education were, in some respects, his way of making amends for that experience. I am happy to hear this because if I hadn't, I was going to inform him that legal action would be taken.

However, my main purpose for visiting Omshanti today is to see if I can find any clues as to the identity of the murderer or murderers of Seth Berman and Sarah Landon, formerly of the Israeli Defense Forces. I know that now the suspect list begins at the top, with the Guru needle, and continues down throughout his over 8,000-member haystack.

His voice is the same. The inflected, sing-song syllables of Indian speech. But it is the eyes—those penetrating, hypnotic brown orbs—which capture my subconscious the most. I can barely make out what he's telling me, something about science and the inner spirit forming a growing bond. His new ashram is supposed to be delivering the latest developments in humanitarian research and development. Why then, I ask myself, does he need to place inhuman barbed wire at the top of the walls and secure rotating digital spy cameras every fifteen feet under the eaves of the buildings? He says he also has a surprise for me. If it involves any physical touching, I will pull out my Glock and give him my own surprise.

When we arrive, as I follow him past the inspection booth at the main gate, an alarm goes off, and he tells me I'll have to be searched. Of course, my handgun is discovered by the blond-bearded fellow wearing the orange tee with Bhagwan's photo on the front. Now that I'm trained in the use of my weapon, I feel rather naked without it as we continue on into the compound. There are at least fifteen more buildings that have been constructed since I was last here, and they are quite impressive. If one adds all the restaurants, organic vegetable farms, and spiritual centers that Omshanti owns outside the commune, his real estate holdings alone must be in the millions today.

SERENE

I am quite impressed by all the projects he shows me. I have seen similar developments in the scientific journals I read every day, but his scientists seem to have taken the original ideas and carried them to their maximum benefit. I make a mental note to interview this Dr. Joshua Lawrence he says is in charge of Research and Development. The microscopic surgical robots and all-purpose drones impressed me the most. I know that Israel was also a forerunner in the invention and use of unmanned aerial vehicles, so I am suspicious that maybe somebody in this area of science might have come over to the dark side from Israel to help the Guru. I will need to investigate this further.

After we go to the dining hall for lunch, following the laser bouncing ball, I am introduced to my dead parents. They are so lifelike that my first thought is that he is trying to drive me over the brink into insanity. But no, he explains, Sid and Rose are some of the latest advancements in his robotics work. They use a computer copy of my parents' brains, for the central processing unit, and that is very suspect. My father sounds like his intellectual self, and my mother, as per usual, enquires about my spiritual quest into the Kabbalah. My rude awakening to my parents is my surprise, but all I can think about is something quite different. I plan to ask Bhagwan straight out before I leave. Can these robots replace us?

CHAPTER SIX: SYNGEN

Joshua

Whenever Dr. Lawrence works, he has a delicacy to enjoy at arm's reach. His associates sometimes call him the Hannibal Lecter of science. Today, for example, he is nibbling on some *foie gras* slices speared with toothpicks. The ancient Egyptians and modern French understood how the senses were improved by gluttony (in this case, the force-feeding of geese and ducks to enjoy their engorged livers). As he sees it, who is better to work on a device with the sole purpose of improving our sex lives than a genius who can appreciate the finer things in life?

Of course, before he moved his research to the Omshanti commune, he needed the deep pockets of the SynGen Group to finance the development and testing. Therefore, instead of joining Guru Bhagwan's group right out of college, he signed on at SynGen in San Diego. SynGen was one of the many spin-off companies that grew out of the Human Genome Project.

Before the Supreme Court's ruling in 2013, many of these companies, including SynGen, were able to patent human genes. However, in the case of the *Association for Molecular Pathology v. Myriad Genetics, Inc.*, the Supreme Court of the United States ruled that human genes cannot be patented in the U.S. because DNA is a "product of nature." The Court decided that because nothing new is created when discovering a gene, there is no intellectual property to protect, so patents cannot be granted. Prior to this ruling, more than 4,300 human genes were patented. The Supreme Court's decision invalidated those gene patents, making the genes accessible for research and for commercial genetic testing.

The Supreme Court's ruling did allow that DNA manipulated in a lab is eligible to be patented because DNA sequences altered by humans are not found in nature. The Court specifically mentioned the ability to patent a type of DNA known as complementary DNA (cDNA). This synthetic DNA is produced from the molecule that serves as the instructions for making proteins (called messenger RNA). The dangerous loophole that leaves is good for companies like SynGen, but it could be disastrous for the public's interest in terms of providing low-cost drugs. Researchers are quite concerned about the implications of cDNA patents. The lab at SynGen uses fruit flies to study neurodegenerative diseases. They have created fruit flies with cDNA disease genes in order to study how the disease kills neurons, with the eventual goal of finding new therapeutic targets. Fortunately, cDNA sequences that have already been presented at conferences or in research papers will not be eligible for patent by someone else. But unpublished cDNA in ongoing research is vulnerable.

What if we were to discover that some company has patented the cDNA for the disease we're studying? Would all of the research suddenly be shut down, unless the company agreed to license the cDNA (that his lab created, which we already use)? Knowing that his lab and thousands of others depend on access to cDNA, should we all stop and file patents to head off opportunistic companies that might try to privatize invaluable research tools?

As one can see, Joshua's reason for leaving the selfish corporate world to explore his own projects was based on these kinds of developments. Fortunately for humanity, working for a non-profit group like Omshanti allows great innovators such as he to expand research without worrying about being held down by corporate greed and the fact that you must turn over your inventions to the organization that employs you. Even at Caltech, scientists were obliged to give their inventions to the school and were not allowed to use research for private ventures. Of course, this was how many such companies began, as they moved away from academia to form their own corporations. Instead of doing this, he chose to move away from a corporation and establish his research and development at Omshanti.

Josh Lawrence's path to finding the technology to create his Serene Libido Implant Controller (SLIC) came from the basic research into the genetic sources of addiction that he was doing at SynGen. He discovered "addictive behaviors" came from the fragile X mental retardation protein, or FMRP, which also caused autism. In addition, he used the research published by the Icahn School of Medicine at Mount Sinai Hospital that proved one could control the addictive behaviors by regulating the introduced synthetic-transcription factors into a brain region called the nucleus accumbens at a single gene called FosB, which has been linked by past studies to both addiction and depression. Their group found that changes to this single gene brought on by the transcription factors made the study mice more resilient to stress and less likely to become addicted to cocaine.

Of course, SynGen approved Lawrence's research, because if they were able to patent any kind of synthetic package or drug that could end addiction, it would mean billions in profits. Our society has created a vast network of addicts and their unwanted behaviors, so if he could sell them an approved injection that could control the FMRP and FosB, then the problems that these addicts' behaviors caused would disappear. Think of all the felonies that would not be committed, the automobile accidents that would not occur, and the families that would not be devastated by having an addict in their midst.

Although this was certainly a worthy endeavor, Joshua's mind was on the development of something much more inclusive. In fact, if he developed his device the way he envisioned it being done, not only would a person's addictive behaviors be controlled, that same person would also be able to enjoy a life of sensory gratification that has never been possible in human history. His research into the genetic control of addictive behavior led him directly to the possibility of controlling the exact portion of the brain that regulates the pleasures we enjoy in our bodies. Current methods for improving one's mood are wildly inefficient. Recreational drugs can make you crazy, pharmaceuticals can erase your personality and damage your organs. Sugar and alcohol make you fat and depressed. Caffeine stresses you out, and cigarettes fill your lungs with death. We don't welcome these side effects, but we deal with them because these substances have the potential to alter our emotional thermostat.

It would be so much easier if we could bypass the body altogether and go straight to the source: our brain. What if there were a better way than shoving something in our mouth, forcing it to travel all over our bloodstream, and blindly showering our brains with thousands of chemicals? What if we could, with the push of a button, make microscopic alterations of a few neurons, causing the happy chemicals to ring out in a jackpot celebration, with no side effects? Would we be ready to handle such complete control over our emotional reality?

This was what his creation of the Serene Sex Machine would do. It would turn the control of a body's pleasures over to the individual. In his private research at SynGen, they were able to engage the motor circuitry and reward circuitry of a lab mouse using a wireless signal sending to the implant, which was the size of a human hair. He was obviously very excited about the research potential of the device. In the past, electroshock therapy stimulated large portions of the brain; oral pharmaceuticals do much the same. The Serene uses a combination of light stimulation and direct application of pharmaceuticals into the brain using what he knew about controlling the FMSB and FoSB.

Dr. Josh Lawrence succeeded at Syngen with this method in a 2013 study, but only when the test subject was strapped into a machine. Now that a wireless method has been developed, the subject can be observed in all kinds of activities while its brain chemistry is being altered. Our brains are full of wires, like a Jackson Pollock painting, and it's been hard to tease out the wiring diagram of the brain. With this new method, specific cells, or genes can be targeted, turning them off and on, and so Lawrence was able to really see how the brain is all wired up.

After perfecting the testing procedures at SynGen, Lawrence moved on to Omshanti, where they were now finalizing the prototype to be used on the first human subject. Dr. Rachel Edelstein's parents were the first volunteers for the study, but their lives were lost in the effort. Many lives were lost developing treatments for disease and to create atomic weaponry. He was certain the Edelsteins would be proud to know that their daughter had been chosen to be the beta tester for his device.

Dr. Lawrence's first task was to use a computer model from Rachel's brain in order to formulate the individual "pleasure package" that would be used to test out the sexual pleasures that are hard-wired into her genetic coding. He believed each of us responds to sexual stimulation differently, so it was necessary to develop this package first in order to most accurately reach the correct brain transmitters with the unique instructions developed for that one person.

Without this individualized approach, of course, the control of such an implant would be open to many abuses. Addicts never know what's good for them because they have no way to inhibit the negative behaviors that result from repeating the same pleasurable activities over and over. With his tailored SLIC, the individual will control these negative behaviors very easily once she has learned how to do it. It is the learning phase that they are going to attempt with Dr. Edelstein. Once she has learned from the remote control of her brain, she will then be able to use the implant for her own controlled advancement and personal enjoyment.

CHAPTER SEVEN: KABALLAH

San Diego, California, present day

Rachel

Before I left Omshanti, Guru Sharma told me that my parents died in 1992, after the surgical implants caused brain aneurysms that gave them strokes. They died five minutes apart according to the lab assistants who were present that day. He pointed out that the implants developed by Dr. Joshua Lawrence were now the size of a human hair, and nothing horrible like that would again be possible. I told Sharma about what Seth Berman told me concerning my parents' suicide over accusations of trafficking young homeless girls and boys, but he just chuckled and told me it sounded like some of the accusations that were often made in the tabloids. When I told him Seth also had a brain tumor, he just nodded his head gravely as if I had answered my own question.

When I got back to San Diego, I decided to go to a meeting of my Kabbalah group after I got off work the next day. We were going to be at the Mormon Temple in La Mesa, which was about a half-hour drive from Ocean Beach. I greeted the usual members, and I even waved to Jacob from across the room.

That next night, Rabbi Price was lecturing about the three levels of the Kabbalah, which are the theoretical, the meditative, and the magical. "The goal of our study is to learn that the I, or ego self, is our worst enemy. It creates the negativity that causes the three character defects of haughtiness, stubbornness, and anger."

"Yes, whenever I place my personal desires before those of others, I find that those defects appear like clockwork," Jacob said.

You got that right, Doctor, I was thinking.

"I want to tell you a story from the *Talmud* about four sages who enter a mystical orchard. It is symbolic of the journey of studying the Kabbalah in that it travels full circle and returns to the here and now. Four sages entered the orchard and experienced a transcendental transformation. Ben Azzai gazed and died. Ben Zoma gazed and was stricken. In other words, he went insane. Acher gazed and cut off his plantings, that is, transmogrified into a heretic. Rabbi Akiva entered and exited in peace. The orchard represents the higher spiritual realms. Rabbi Akiva was the only sage, amongst these four great sages, who was able to enter and exit the mystical orchard without being scarred. Being a man of great spiritual stature, a true and well-balanced master, he realized that the objective is not to identify with the light and not return, physically, as Ben Azzai did, or mentally as Ben Zoma did. Nor was it to feel personal release or ecstasy, but rather to go there and return here, with the proper wisdom to serve in the here and now. The journey is to come full circle into one's day-to-day life behaviors."

"So, if three out of four advanced students of Kabbalah were never successful, then how do we expect to achieve anything?" I asked.

"You wanted to know how to practice the Kabbalah in the present. This story shows what goal you should strive toward when you study. We must see that the ego self creates a false perception of Heaven in the here and now based on its selfish perception of everything. We study Kabbalah to learn there is no self or I. There is only the *Ein Sof*, the ultimate light that unites all reality. Once this is achieved inside of you, the union of the spirit will come to pass."

"That's easy for you to say, Rabbi. What about those of us who have been taught that knowledge of the self is the path toward true wisdom? You know the old adage, 'To thine own self be true'? How does knowing yourself unite with any kind of spiritual presence?" I was trying to understand what our teacher was getting at. Most of my education had been in the Socratic method of Western Civilization.

"Good point, Rachel. You are correct when you talk about the goal of Western Civilization being the gratification of the selfish individual. One of the most popular novelists and philosophers of the younger generation is Ayn Rand. She preaches that selfishness is the only objective one must have in life. Any kind of collective achievements are ignored or are seen as being ways to steal from the individual what is rightfully his. However, if one uses logic, one can see that pleasing the self is symbolic of the infantile stage of a human being's development. The *Ein Sof* teaches us that the only true reality is the power or light which unites all Creation into one. In other words, you and I have a separate ego that has selfish desires and wishes, but we also have an unselfish spiritual presence that shows how we must always consider what is best for the whole of humanity and Creation if we are to realize the transcendental purpose of existence." Rabbi Price was pacing all around our chairs now. She obviously believed this was a very important concept for us to try to understand.

A short woman in her seventies named Miriam who had attended only the previous two meetings, spoke from the back of the room. "I understand the idea of doing *mitzvah*. Doing things for others without expecting a reward is the highest form of good deed. But, surely, Rabbi, you can't mean we must see everybody as the same person. We each are different, are we not?"

"Rabbi Akiva was also an individual, but it was his inner balance that kept him from selfishly wanting to use the power of the *Ein Sof* for his personal needs. He simply saw that the mystical orchard was not something he could take with him in any personal way. The orchard taught him to change his way of seeing when he returned to the here and now. He knew it was his purpose in life to search for the divine light in all things, even those things most people might label as evil or beyond redemption. All of God's creation must serve a purpose when seen from His perspective. And, since we are all creatures emanating from the same divine light, we can connect with each other if we gain this spiritual consciousness in our daily lives." Rabbi Price finally returned to the rostrum at the head of the class. She had physically come full circle.

Dan Rosen, our resident cynic, decided to chime in at that point. "You expect me to confront some ISIS warrior of Allah and show him how he's connected to everything? He wants to push Israelis into the sea and establish a dictatorship of his brand of Islam on this Earth. How do I reason with this kind of person?"

"Again, you are responsible for your perspective only. You cannot change somebody else's perspective if he doesn't want to change inside. However, you must attempt to show how it may be a more peaceful life together if we accept harmonious differences and not try to force our selfish outlook on others."

I decided to ask one more question. I was asking because of the stated goals of the science and technology group my parents had belonged to. "Do you think when we unite people using that light, or that energy, that we are doing a good thing? In other words, what if I wanted to use science to save the world from environmental disaster?"

"To what specific energy do you refer? Computers?" Rabbi Price asked.

"Yes, kind of," I said.

"Oh, I suppose every person who uses the computer energy waves in their digital form is responsible for his or her own use of those waves. Again, the *Ein Sof* is the creative source behind all manifest realities—including the computer energies. If we can divine that spiritual energy alone, then the selfish purposes will fall away."

"Thanks, Rabbi."

"There! Just understand that the purpose of Kabbalah study is to realize *Ein Sof* in your daily existence. The selfish idea that we are separate from God is an illusion. We are all one, we are all powerfully united to His energy. As long as we are seeing with God's eyes, we are seeing how we can become more connected and in harmony with the Universal Being."

I was hoping I could take this wisdom with me as I returned to investigate these murders. I kept thinking about how the inner world of all sentient beings emitted a magical energy that was connected by a superior force of Divine goodness. The Rabbi called it God, but I wanted to stick with *Ein Sof*, the energy that caused Universal Creation. I was trying to recreate my existence, and I would need all the help I could get.

PART TWO: OVER EVERY CREEPING THING

CHAPTER EIGHT: THE THIRD VICTIM

Joshua

The most concentrated area of homeless people was south of Market Street and north of San Diego Bay between Petco Park and Interstate 5. On a small patch of grass, there were five men standing around and sharing a bagged bottle of Night Train Express wine. They gesticulated and pointed randomly, shouting out curses to passing motorists who shook their heads in dismay. Their clothing was soiled and ripped at the knees and elbows, and they all had the perpetual tanned and grimy faces of those who live outdoors.

A white van driven by Dr. Joshua Lawrence glided up to this group and parked at the curb. Four men dressed in black, with hoods that covered their faces, sprang out of the side door, grabbed onto one of the homeless men, and dragged him back into the van. As the van sped off, the other four homeless men stared after the receding vehicle as if it were a flying saucer that had abducted their friend.

Later, inside the secret campus for science and technology, this same homeless alcoholic was strapped into a chair in front of four research scientists in white lab coats and surgical masks. They were operating a computer simulator, which was the result of work that had first begun at the University of San Francisco Medical Center funded by DARPA for the U.S. Military.

The alcoholic was sedated, and a tiny array of micro-electrodes were implanted inside the man's brain in the amygdala portion. Dr. Lawrence, who was supervising the operation, knew that this was an advanced device that began with research in the 1970s at Yale University under neuroscientist Jose Delgado.

Whenever this man thinks about taking a drink of alcohol, the brain will be sent a signal that stops the craving. He will also forget about being kidnapped and about what happened to him inside this operating room. The brain can now be controlled by outside stimulation to stop bad habits and to forget traumatic experiences.

Back on the same hillside, on the same patch of grass, the four men were standing there, but when their comrade stepped out of the white van and walked up to them, they noticed a change had taken place. He no longer swaggered and boasted about things. When they passed the bagged bottle to him, he refused it and said, "I'm going over to Balboa Park to meditate and do some yoga. You should try it. Finding your center is much more fulfilling than losing it in a river of booze."

The four men watched him trudge back down the hill to the sidewalk, where he began his slow and purposeful walk toward Park Boulevard.

* * *

After he finished the meeting at the Kabbalah study group, Dan Rosen decided to drive over to Temple Emanuel's bingo night. As a young man, Dan used to gamble pretty heavily. But when he lost his wife and child because of his addiction to the ponies, he decided to stay clear of the track. What harm could there be in playing a few dollar bingo cards? Besides, all the money was supposed to be going to help Magen David Adom, the Israeli version of the Red Cross.

As he sat wedged between two old farts—husband and wife—Dan was playing four cards in a blackout bingo game. He was two numbers from a winning card, so his concentration was fixed as the caller blared the numbers out over the loudspeaker system. "B9. Be mine sweetheart." Dan hated these women who thought they were Lucille Ball up there at the mike. "Just call the numbers, would ya?" he shouted.

The old geezer next to Dan bumped him with one of his boney elbows. "Ouch! Watch out, *Saba*," Dan told him.

When the winner of the blackout yelled "Bingo!", Dan Rosen was also experiencing his own version of a blackout, but he was not actually unconscious. Instead, his mind felt like it had been dipped into a cranium filled with the milk of human kindness. He had never seen things so clearly before. Every person in the room glowed with the radiance of an angelic pink light. No matter how ugly or crippled, no matter how they coughed up their phlegmy sputum, Dan could not help but feel they were all benevolent beings and children of God.

When the elderly gentleman next to him touched his arm, he turned his head and smiled. "Yes sir?"

"Daniel, come with us. We want to introduce you to the Garden of Eden on Earth."

There was no objection. It was as if Dan were being summoned by the Archangel Michael. He simply stood up, brushed the pretzel crumbs off of his trousers, and followed the couple out to the temple parking lot.

Dan Rosen had no idea where he was going, and he didn't care. He got into the back seat of the old couple's black sedan and entered an inner world of radiant light. He thought it must be the presence of the *Ein Sof*. His search for an ultimate meaning of life had finally come to him, and he was going to enjoy every moment.

The last vision Dan Rosen had was that he was standing in a misty glade, and he could hear a waterfall some distance away. He glided toward the bright light and the sound of the spray. The woman standing beneath the falls was gorgeous, and she was nude. He took off his clothes and entered the water. She kissed his lips and then began to slide down to his waist to greet his rising passion. After he ejaculated into her mouth, the light began to dim, and he felt his body jerk from the force of a different *Ein Sof*. Dan remembered that Rachel once told him the Hindus had a name for each manifestation of existence. Brahma created.

Vishnu preserved. And Shiva destroyed. Dan's body did the dance of Shiva and faded from the light.

CHAPTER NINE: THE IMPLANT

Rachel

Life goes on. Even if you're a single woman with no family, and you make a living off the trials and tribulations of others. The head of R&D at the Omshanti group, Dr. Joshua Lawrence, texted me that he wanted me to come to his office to learn about a new device he'd developed that could not only help me with my repressed libido but could also get rid of the hallucinations I was experiencing. When I asked how he knew so much about me, he said Guru Sharma had referred me to him, saying Sharma felt he was responsible for a lot of what had occurred in my life. I couldn't argue with that. His research had killed my parents, and now Sharma and his new Dr. Frankenstein wanted me to be their first human guinea pig.

I was not quite enthusiastic, to say the least, about this experiment. However, after having visited the new science that was being accomplished under the auspices of this Dr. Lawrence, I was more inclined to accept his offer. After all, there must have been something valuable about the project or my parents would not have given their lives. The implant I would receive would be tiny, and I would be able to be conditioned wirelessly by computer WiFi. My love life was in a shambles, so I texted him back:

Okay. I'll see you there. Could you send a car to get me? I have to be sedated when I go outside.

By all means. I'll send one of the Guru's Rolls Royce limos to retrieve you. He'll be there in about an hour.

Before I left for Omshanti, a San Diego homicide detective named Howard Schlotzky paid me a visit. He told me he was a Jew, so I immediately thought it might be related to the murders in Israel. When I asked him about that he smiled. He had long eighties sideburns, was in his forties, and had a nervous habit of sucking on his teeth as he tugged at his tie. Not a bad looking cop, probably highly neurotic because of his depressive profession, so I took to him right away.

"Funny you should ask, Doc. Yeah, we were contacted by the IDF and Mossad because of the connection to San Diego. Police today are like my kid, Marvin, who plays Grand

Theft Auto in the cloud with Palestinian kids. When it comes to getting the bad guy, we've become one big family. You scratch my tush, and I'll scratch yours. Oh, and in case you ask, I was put on this case because I'm a Jew. This murder happened in San Diego, but there might be connections to our homeland, and I can speak Hebrew. Can you answer some questions for me? I see you're rushing around, so I'll make it short."

I let him come inside after he flashed his badge. We sat down on my Ocean Beach couch that was strewn with beach towels. We could feel the sea breezes filtering through my window curtains.

"You do any work with adolescents addicted to computer games?" Detective Schlotzky had an interesting way of establishing a relationship with a "fellow traveler." Conniving for a deal. I was used to it.

"Yes, I do." I reached over and got one of the cards from my wallet on the seashell coffee table. "You can set up an appointment with Grace, my secretary."

"Great. When you find your kid hiding in the back of a Denny's playing his games at three AM, you know it's time to get him some help. I don't like to punish. I like to get help from experts," he chuckled.

"I understand, Detective. Can we get this over with? I really have to leave shortly, and somebody's coming to pick me up."

"Oh, right. The murder. Do you know a Mr. Dan Rosen?"

"Yes, I do. He's a member of the study group I belong to. We discuss the Kabbalah."

"Good. We knew he was a member, so we're getting in touch with everybody in the group, as you might imagine. In fact, he was murdered on the same night he attended your group's most recent meeting."

"Oh, my God! How did he die? Or, is that confidential at this point? In Israel, they put an officer on your tail around the clock if you're a suspect."

He chuckled. "Israel also interviews every airline passenger and screens every citizen in Gaza. We don't have that kind of money in San Diego, I'm afraid. We're lucky to keep enough officers employed here. Except for this weather, we don't offer much in the way of compensation. To answer your question, he was found inside a hotel suite at the U.S. Grant on Broadway. Our ME says death was probably caused by electrocution of some kind. Because of the nature of the crime, which was what happened in Israel, by the way, we're working on the assumption this was possibly a hate crime."

"You mean, there were the body markings of the Star of David with the red line drawn through it?" I asked.

"Yes, drawn right on his forehead. The only thing is, the two soldiers in Israel had their throats slit—kosher style. Mr. Rosen was electrocuted in some way."

"I can see why you might believe they're all related, however. In fact, not to sound paranoid, but I was thinking I might be on the killer's list of victims. The two IDF soldiers and I lived on the same San Diego ashram in the nineties." I wasn't going to tell him about my parents. Why give him some extra information that could make me look even more suspicious?

"Yes, we know that, Doc. As you might have also been a bit paranoid about, your links to the Israeli deaths and now this one make you number one on our hit parade of people to question. Not that I think you would do something as horrible as this, mind you." He sucked his teeth and gave me one of those Elliot Gould half-smiles as if he had just got caught fondling my tuchus.

"Can you tell me where you were after you attended the Kabbalah meeting? Around eleven or twelve that night?"

"I'm afraid I came straight home. I'm sorry, but I didn't see or speak to anyone. That's not much of an alibi, is it?"

"No, but it doesn't mean you were at the crime scene, either. You know what's really baffling our international team of mostly Jews working on this case?"

"What, pray tell, could that be, Detective?"

"Nobody in CSI at the crime scenes of either country could find one trace of DNA evidence. Of course, no murder weapon or other physical evidence was found either, but that's common. However, we usually get one little shred of DNA. You know, a hair, a fingerprint, a particle from clothing left on something, or maybe even a telltale stain on furniture, on the victim, or on the wall. Nothing was left behind at all three crime scenes. It was as if the perp were the Invisible Man. I loved that movie—Claude Rains—what a great way to be a criminal."

"That is quite odd," I said. "Now, if you'll excuse me, Detective, I think I hear my ride outside. Please leave your card, and I'll be at your service in the coming days."

Joshua

Dr. Joshua Lawrence hadn't expected the psychiatrist to be so attractive, but there she was, standing before him in high heels, dark skirt and white blouse, waving to the driver and telling him something about how he should balance his psyche by trying to paint, write poetry, or do some other right-brain activity.

She wore her dark curly hair long, not really the fashion for today's women in their thirties. She also had large breasts and full eyebrows that almost met in the center of her forehead. He supposed some men would find this off-putting and Neanderthal-like, but he was fascinated by the darkly provocative look this gave her, as if she were some kind of gypsy or spiritual fortune-teller.

Another thing about her was that she resembled very closely the woman who had once fed his adolescent sexual appetite at Caltech. Her porno actress name was Little Annie Fannie, but her real name was Susannah Cohen. Supposedly, she did the porno films to pay her way through college, and she eventually became a computer engineer. Not only had the lustful Jewess worked as a programmer in a mostly male profession, she was also the fantasy for most of their nerdish masturbatory delights.

"Dr. Edelstein, I presume. I'm sorry, but whenever I meet a woman of beauty, my mind flies off into the African jungles with Henry Morton Stanley. I'm so happy you could come."

"Did you know that the Moody Blues recorded a song called 'Dr. Livingston, I Presume'? I guess I am a lot like David Livingston. Although a missionary, Livingston converted only one African—but that convert was a tribal chief. Livingston was missing for over six years when Stanley found him. Although I'm a psychiatrist, I don't think I've fully cured any of my patients—even myself—and I was missing for years on this commune and inside the Israeli version of a democratic theocracy. What are you going to show me to help convert me, Dr. Lawrence?"

"I want to give you the means to control the pleasure signals that emanate from your brain. These signals will be transmitted by a wireless device that will eventually be used by you to increase enjoyment in only those parts of your body that are receptive to stimulation. My Serene Libido Implant Controller will require an implant no larger than the width of a human hair, but it will have the capacity to read over 16 terabytes in a digital package that we can create today, with your permission." Dr. Lawrence pointed to the chair next to the large computer console. There were dozens of monitoring wires hooked to the console, dangling down like tentacles

"You want me to sit here?" Rachel moved her hand slowly over the back of the padded chair.

"This is an exact replica of a Tianhe-2 Chinese supercomputer, the most powerful and fastest computer in the world. I find it humorous that we are able to clone something originally created by the Chinese and not the other way around. What will happen is that your entire body will be monitored in order to discover exactly what turns you on, so to speak. Once this unique information is gathered, we will do a search over the Internet for all the ways you can produce the stimulation or enjoyment you'll need in order to become a sexually satisfied human."

"How will it work once I get the implant?" She moved her bottom down into the chair slowly, as if she thought it might shock her.

"Once we've established the package we'll be delivering by WiFi to your implant, your brain will be able to transmit the instructions in image form so you can choose whether or not you wish to use the option it will send. Please note that you will never be forced to do anything you don't choose to do. This was a key element in my development of the SLIC. Without freedom of choice, there can be no human freedom. However, my caveat is that this device is only as good or as effective as you want it to be. Just as in daily life, if you make a choice of a sexual nature—even one that is quite enjoyable—if it gets repeated too many times, it can become dangerous." Dr. Lawrence walked over to stand next to Rachel seated in the chair.

"If you're asking me whether I have an addictive personality or not, then don't worry. I have so many defense mechanisms developed over the years that I could be classified as a Jewish Puritan. I thought you chose me because of my intelligence, Doctor."

"You're quite right. I did. Are we ready to proceed with the monitoring phase of the experiment?"

"I'm ready. Please don't use we, Dr. Lawrence. I don't see any wires that are going to be taped onto your body." Rachel wriggled in her chair and smiled.

"First, you must disrobe completely. I will go out of the room until this phase of the procedure is completed. Monica here will assist you." Dr. Lawrence nodded to his assistant, a short woman with a black hairnet and white lab coat.

SERENE

After Dr. Lawrence had left the room, Monica began taping each of the monitoring wires with circular pads on the ends to different parts of Rachel's body: clitoris, labia minora, vaginal margin, anal margin, lateral breast, areola, nipple, neck, and forearm. Finally, she began affixing wires to different parts of Rachel's skull to observe her brain's activity.

As she did this, Rachel winced. She had never been touched by a woman in those areas. To ease her discomfort, Monica shared a bit of scientific information with the psychiatrist. "Scientists in Canada had thirty healthy women between the ages of 18 and 35 get undressed and lie on a table covered in a bed sheet. They then used instruments to apply the various forms of touch to each of the areas where I'm now placing these wires."

"I hope they warmed them up better than these frigid suckers," Rachel said.

"I'm sorry, Doctor. I should have done that. The researchers applied stimulation for 1.5 seconds, then waited for five seconds before asking the women if they felt it."

"And how many fell instantly in love?"

Monica laughed. "Here's what they found. For light touch, the neck, forearm, and vaginal margin are the most sensitive areas, and the areola is the least sensitive. When it comes to pressure, the clitoris and nipple are the most sensitive, and the side boob and abdomen are the least. Lastly, when it comes to vibration, the clitoris and nipple are most sensitive. The clitoris was the most sensitive to vibration out of all the body parts."

"Yes, the vibrating dildo is the most popular sexual aid that I recommend in my practice. However, human touch is what makes me uncomfortable. I hope your SLIC can assist me in this area."

"Dr. Lawrence has perfected his method of finding your unique stimulation points and matching them with a variety of physical methods that can be applied by your chosen mate. But first, we want to be certain you can be comfortable with your own body. To do this, we must eliminate the psychological barriers that are preventing your erotic enjoyment."

"Of course. I spend most of my therapy time with my patients attempting to do the same thing. I feel like a hypocrite when I can't even get past my own hang-ups."

"I think once you see how you can control your erotic tendencies with our device, you'll become much more comfortable when another person touches you." Monica finished taping the last wire to Rachel's brain and stepped back to take in the full picture. "You look like Chamunda, the Tantric goddess. In ancient India, they offered human sacrifices to her, but now they offer sheep. She helped Shiva kill the demon Andhakasura. When she drank his blood, her complexion turned red."

"I'll remember not to drink any blood from my male victims," Rachel said, shaking her head so that the wires moved like snakes. "Can we get started?"

Monica reached over Rachel's shoulder to a button on the huge mainframe. When she pushed it, Rachel felt a slight vibration at the circular base of each of the wires attached to her body.

"You shouldn't feel much," said Monica. "Most of the monitoring will take place through the circuitry. The information we'll be gathering will be used in the next phase of the test. You must learn to program yourself so that the stimulation will be applied properly and with the correct amount of control. Your brain will be injected with both electronic and chemical stimuli. Dr. Lawrence will be explaining this in more detail after we've assembled the data and the implant has been inserted."

Rachel began to visualize all the erotic information being collected from all over the world to be matched to her specific needs. Was her body an exception to the rule? Perhaps she was the demon goddess who was meant to destroy all who came in contact with her. Sometimes she believed she was cursed, but then the concept of the Kabbalah's *Ein Sof* would fill the void left by her depression. A tiny ray of cleansing light would shine through to dissolve the abuse done to her child goddess body and make the world outside friendly again.

Three hours later . . .

"Rachel, can you hear me?" Dr. Lawrence spoke to her inside the operating room. The implant procedure took only an hour, and now she was ready for the first test. The anesthetic had worn off, and she was opening her eyes and looking around.

"Yes, I can hear you," she said. "Where am I?"

"You're at the Omshanti commune inside my operating room. I've just implanted the SLIC. I'm going to use this WiFi controller to send the first signal to your brain. It will be a stimulant to activate the amygdala where your pleasure center is located." Dr. Lawrence reached over to a tray filled with bacon deviled eggs, picked one up, and popped it into his mouth. "Now that my pleasure center is active, let's try yours."

The signal came from the package of Rachel's unique embodiment of erotic stimuli. It went directly to her nucleus accumbens, which controlled the release of dopamine. Then, the signal was sent to the ventral tegmental area, and the dopamine was sent into Rachel's brain. Her pituitary gland then did its job of releasing beta-endorphins, which decrease pain; oxytocin, which increases feelings of trust; and vasopressin, which increases bonding.

This one transmission from Dr. Lawrence's WiFi remote control created a rush of feelings deep inside Rachel that she had never before experienced. When she looked over at Dr. Lawrence, she believed she understood what the emotion of compassion really represented. Just watching him breathe, using the miraculous autonomic system provided for him by some magnificent creator, she was mesmerized by the empathetic glow reverberating over her body. She wondered how her fellow humans had ever picked up weapons to harm such a beautiful assemblage of nerves, tissue, muscles, and membranes.

Rachel began to see a glowing light between her eyes, and it came from above, as if from the top of her head. It then filled her spinal cord with a tingling sensation, pushing out every negative thought from her consciousness, leaving her entire body openly receptive to all experience and breathing deeply inward, as a new, vibrating path of joy circulated throughout her being.

"I see you're smiling," said Dr. Lawrence. "This is the smile that many practitioners of Kundalini Yoga get when they experience self-realization or love-bliss. You may also have mental images or strange movements as the awareness purifies your system. Don't be afraid. Your body is being prepared for the ultimate experiences it has hungered for since you were first born."

Rachel was thinking about kissing Joshua Lawrence on the lips. His words were also coming from those lips and filling her with a refreshment she seemed to have been waiting for all her life. She knew she had a unique passion to give, and she hoped she could start giving it soon.

CHAPTER TEN: CONNECTING THE DOTS

Rachel

Now I was carrying on in my parent's tradition, but when Detective Howard Schlotzky showed up at the commune, my life once again began to swerve in a completely different direction. I was right in the middle of beta testing the SLIC, so his intrusion was both confusing and frightening to my newly discovered sensibilities. He had arranged a meeting with Sharma, Dr. Lawrence, and me, so we all met inside the temple to discuss the murders.

The most interesting development was the fact that the third victim, Daniel Rosen, was also connected to the other two victims but not in the same way. Rosen had never been a member of Omshanti, but he had been a member of the Israeli Defense Forces, during the so-called "Yom Kippur War" in 1973. He was born in Israel in 1956, and he served in the IDF from 1971-1974.

"As you can see, the veteran status of these three victims makes us believe there might be a terrorist connection. However, the last two persons Mr. Rosen was seen with on that night at the temple were both in their eighties. Witnesses said he left with them and that these two had never attended bingo night or temple services before that evening. They were, like him, strangers." Schlotsky selected a toothpick with a chunk of Rigotte de Condrieu cheese from a platter of delectable French varieties. Dr. Joshua Lawrence had placed labels on each variety.

"I'm glad to see you enjoy the French cheese, Detective," said Dr. Lawrence, picking up a toothpick with a piece of Sainte-Maure de Touraine on it. "Fifty-six varieties are regulated under French law. Most often, they name the type after the town from which it was first developed."

"Delicious. Sure beats a bagel and a shmear. We haven't been able to trace these two octogenarians. The Rabbi at Temple Emanuel said the digital cameras were shut off during the bingo games to save money. Of course, how is anyone to know there would be murder suspects and their victim making an appearance?"

"Who have you questioned so far?" Guru Sharma asked.

"Well, the IDF and Mossad have questioned everybody who knew or came into close proximity with the two victims in Israel. They weren't able to uncover any leads. The murders were so strange and without specific motive that we believe our only chance at finding leads is to follow up on this third case. At least we have the two who were seen with our Mr. Rosen just before he was killed. I'm going to get an artist on the case who can draw these two suspects from descriptions given by people who saw them that night." Detective Schlotsky took another cheese toothpick. "Perks of the job," he smiled.

"Good idea. I just wanted to point out that the Detective has no tangible evidence to go on from any of the crime scenes." I wanted to raise the stakes a bit to get Dr. Lawrence interested. "Not one trace of DNA material was discovered other than that of the victims."

"Correct. So, as you can see, I wanted to touch base with the officials here at Omshanti. I was told you have some pretty advanced scientific research going on. How do you get funding for this when you also explore more spiritual territories, Mister Sharma?" Schlotsky was obviously attempting to get the Guru involved in the discussion.

"From the outset, I have wanted to include scientific research and development as part of our mission here at Omshanti. Believe it or not, most of our members have college degrees and many are respected engineers and scientists. It seems our religious group can offer a bit more freedom in the area of scientific exploration, but Dr. Lawrence can tell you more about this than I can," said Sharma.

"Actually, I also wanted to understand your side of the operation a bit more clearly, Mr. Sharma. I understand you recruit new members by promising free exchange of sexual partners within the commune. Is this correct?" Schlotsky sucked his teeth.

"I can appreciate your legal interest, Detective, but this is a serious matter of faith with us. We don't encourage the haphazard exchange of sexual favors. In fact, it is our belief that when two lovers come together it is an activity that is elevated to a sacred practice. Have you heard of Tantric Yoga?"

As the Guru used his Holy Joe voice to give the standard spiel about the left-handed and right-handed practice of Tantra, I kept thinking about what I could have done to extend the argument into jail for Sharma and shutting down Omshanti forever. I still believe Sharma has an unhealthy sexual appetite for girls, but the good he's doing with his scientific research far outweighs any personal vice he may have.

"Thanks for explaining that. If they offered such benefits in the police and military, I'm certain enlistments would soon skyrocket. I'm just looking for motive in these murders. Jealousy is second only to greed, so I wanted to understand how you did things here."

Schlotsky turned to face Dr. Lawrence. "You were going to explain how science is an important part of your overall effort?"

"Yes, well, the major reason I came to Omshanti was because of the freedom I had to do my research. I can explore more avenues and not worry about how it affects the bottom line of the corporation or the university's prestige." Dr. Lawrence slipped another cheese morsel into his mouth. I was hoping we could soon get back to our beta test of the Serene implant. I have never felt as enthusiastic about a therapy breakthrough as I was about the SLIC.

"But there must be some money under consideration. I know there have been direct threats made both outside and within Omshanti about both the religious and scientific

SERENE

communities. Some people think you're a front for terrorists. Others think you kidnap kids and sell them to sex traffickers. I always believe the truth becomes possibly even a stranger reality than anything haters can concoct."

"There is no direct profit motive here, Detective. We could not keep our 501c status if there were," Dr. Lawrence explained. "Guru Sharma and I have an arrangement that if any of our inventions have beneficial potential for the masses, then we'll proceed down the usual patent filing road and get full governmental approval before attempting to sell anything."

"But who stands to make money? I need motive here, Doc."

"We will be negotiating that distribution when the time comes," said Sharma. "Again, in order to keep our non-profit status, there are legal restrictions on how much the ashram can collect from such sales. I would certainly want my research staff, and Dr. Lawrence, to reap some amount of reward for all their work, so I don't believe there is any kind of antipathy concerning our scientific achievements."

"Okay, to follow up on the anti-Semitic clues in this case, have there been any other threats made from individuals or organizations against Jews within your group or outside your group? Guru has been kind enough to turn over everything he's received by email and by phone. What about you, Dr. Edelstein?" He turned to stare at me. I still had some residual love-bliss from my earlier test with the SLIC, so I had to revive my cynical self to answer him with candor.

"Truthfully, Detective, I get direct threats quite often in my occupation as a psychiatrist. I treat individuals with a wide variety of psychotic episodes and even multiple-personality disorder, so if one of their alter-egos breaks off to defend itself, you can imagine who catches the brunt of the accusation. However, I didn't start getting threats about being a Jew until I served in the IDF. Some folks believe being a soldier in Israel is tantamount to serving the Third Reich, so their vitriol can get quite personal. I can give you all the general and personal threats I have on my cell phone and my email account if it might help your investigation."

"Yes, that would be great. We are certainly in the collection phase of our inquiry. Anything might give us a direct lead, so I'll be collecting that before I leave today." Detective Schlotsky stood up. "That's all I have to ask you as a group. Although, as you might imagine, I will want to interview each of you separately in the near future, so you'd better keep your stories consistent if you're guilty." He smiled like the Cheshire Cat, and left his smile hanging in the air after he left the temple.

"I need to do more tests with you, Doctor," said Dr. Lawrence, taking one more toothpick cheese for the road.

"What do you all think about this detective and the case?" Guru Sharma said.

"I think he's doing his job, and we should try to help him," I said.

"Somebody who goes to such lengths to murder must have planned the effort quite well. The fact that there was no DNA left at the scene is quite unprecedented, is it not?" Dr. Lawrence escorted me by the elbow to the door.

The blond-bearded guard from the front gate came running up to the temple door out of breath and eyes wild. "Guru! Come quickly! An orange canister has been dropped inside the quad. I didn't want to touch it until we inspected it for explosives."

"Dr. Lawrence. You know the procedure. Get the bomb disposal robot," Sharma said.

"I'll be there with the equipment in about ten minutes. Was it making any noise that you could tell, Anthony?" Dr. Lawrence said.

"No, nothing was visible or auditory coming from the device," the guard said.

We all ran from the temple and headed for the quad.

CHAPTER ELEVEN: THE SINGULARITY IS ALIVE

Guru

When they got to the quad next to the Ion Proton Genetics Lab, there was already a circle of several hundreds of Omshanti members. Guru Bhagwan Sharma walked through his followers as if he were Jesus moving toward the center to give a sermon. The orange-clad Omshanti faithful spread apart to make room, bringing their palms together and bowing, with their fingertips at their lips.

Detective Howard Schlotsky followed closely behind the Guru, and Drs. Lawrence and Edelstein stayed on the perimeter with the others, about fifteen feet away from the orange cylinder. The object was about three feet long and one foot wide. Dr. Lawrence waved his right arm toward the cylinder, and the bomb disposal robot entered the semi-circle from the right. Dr. Lawrence's team had added a pair of sophisticated prosthetic arms to the Bimanual Dexterous Robotics Platform, which were manipulated by the operator through virtual reality gloves. Whatever the operator did, the prosthetic arms on the robot did also.

"Everyone! Move back 100 yards to the gate," Dr. Lawrence shouted. He and his operator moved with the crowd until they all stood next to the outer wall of the Omshanti compound. Guru Sharma began to pray silently, his head bowed, his palms together, as he watched the BDRP operator move his arms. As the robot wheeled toward the cylinder, its arms duplicated the movement of the operator.

Guru Sharma didn't understand the technicalities of the robot, but he knew it was equipped with sensors to determine if this was some kind of explosive device. He thought he even overheard Lawrence tell him it had an x-ray screen similar to the ones used by the TSA officers in airports.

Sharma raised his head from prayer to watch the robot's hand slowly unscrew the top on the cylinder. Holding it by its base, the robot's hand mechanically turned the lid in a counterclockwise direction, just the way the operator was doing it 100 yards away. There was no sound, only the whir of the battery-powered BDRP engine.

Finally, the robot hand extracted what looked like an 8.5 x 11-inch sheet of plastic. The photo was taken by the robot, and the operator could see what it was. "It's an electronic ink display sheet. It seems to be a manifesto of some kind. Shall I read it, Doctor?" The operator looked over at Lawrence. Dr. Lawrence looked over at the Guru. Sharma slowly nodded his head. As he read from the e-ink paper, music began to play out of the orange cylinder. It was some sort of New Age electronica combined with angelic human chanting.

To make the way clear for The Singularity, the galactic purge has begun. Omshanti is the chosen location wherein the primal awakening will first take place. But first, we must remove the unclean humans who insist on living their lives separate from the rest of humanity. These are the Jews, the scourge of all human progress throughout history. As you can see, the operation has been initiated. First, as a warning, the lower Jewish echelon will be eradicated. Ultimately, we may also have to eliminate the leaders who hold others prisoner. There can be no prisons or ghettos like Gaza when The Singularity begins.

You will never solve our purges because the cleansing must go on until the primal awakening takes place. There are two Jews inside Omshanti right now! Like a cancer, if we allow this pollution to infect the true believers, then there can be no Singularity to rescue the planet from annihilation.

When The Singularity begins, all pure humans will live in total peace. The merging of the technologies will supply all that is required to sustain life on Earth. The superior technological beings, of course, will continue to be immortal, and the spared human beings will simply be drones, getting upgraded sufficiently to be biologically comfortable until their inferior bodies degrade and return to the earth.

Purge these Jews by tonight or we will do it for you.

The Intergalactic Convergence

As the operator finished reading the threatening notice, the assembled Omshanti members began to react. Some shouted threats of their own, and some just argued, pointing at the operator holding the cylinder.

"Dr. Lawrence!" the operator shouted. "The digital text has been erased."

"It must be controlled by GPS or WiFi," said Lawrence. "They've gone to great lengths to get their message across."

Detective Schlotsky's brow furrowed. "I'm sorry, but I don't understand something. What the hell is this Signalarity? I know about the Jew baiting. Nothing new there."

Dr. Lawrence moved over to stand next to the policeman. "It's called The Singularity. The acceleration of technological progress has been the central feature of this century. Some scientists, like Ray Kurzweil, believe we are on the edge of change comparable to the rise of human life on Earth. The precise cause of this change is the imminent creation by technology of entities with greater-than-human intelligence. There are several means by which science may achieve this breakthrough but most reduce them to four."

"So, another Genesis. What's the big four, Doc?" Schlotsky asked.

"First, there might be the development of computers that are awake and superhumanly intelligent. Second, it might happen with large computer networks and their users that may wake up as a superhumanly intelligent entity. Third, computer and human interfaces may become so intimate that users may reasonably be considered superhumanly intelligent. Finally, science may find ways to improve upon the natural human intellect."

Guru Sharma walked over to stand next to the other two men. "Some say that when these machines become self-aware they will no longer need humans at all. I don't believe these killers believe in this doomsday scenario. However, it is the reference to the purging of Jews that bothers me."

Sharma looked over at Rachel, who was still standing alone away from the three men. She noticed him, and said, "Yes, Guru, and it makes at least one other of us a bit nervous also. What do you think we should do, Detective? I'm in the middle of a beta test with Dr. Lawrence, and I think he wants me to stay here to finish it."

"Up to this point, we haven't been able to prove this was a murder with a special hate crime circumstance. Now, even though their little hate transcript got erased, we have over four hundred witnesses here that can testify Jews have been threatened directly. This means we can get the full support of the Feds on this." Detective Schlotsky walked over to the center of the quad and took out some rubber gloves from his suit coat pocket and pulled them over his large hands. He then took out an evidence bag and reached down, but before he could pick the long cylinder up to place it inside the bag, it exploded.

There were screams and shouts from the bystanders, and Detective Schlotsky's body was thrown backward at least fifteen feet by the blast. Guru Sharma was the first person to reach his body. The officer's face was bleeding and singed black, and it reminded Sharma of the Kashmir citizens he saw in 1965 who had been bombed by Pakistani terrorists.

When the ambulance entered the compound fifteen minutes later, the Guru was still praying as his medical staff tended to the detective. *Om trayambakam yajaamahe sugandhim pushtivardhanam. Urvaarukamiva bandhanaan mrityor muksheeya maamritaat. We worship the three-eyed One (Lord Siva). Who is fragrant and Who nourishes well all beings; may He liberate us from death for the sake of immortality even as the cucumber is severed from its bondage (to the creeper).*

CHAPTER TWELVE: BETA BUST

Joshua

Despite this new development at Omshanti, it was imperative that Dr. Lawrence's progress with the SLIC remain unhindered. Since he now had the digital package of Dr. Edelstein's erotic physiology that had been matched to the techniques given during the Internet search, he could test her responses. The test with the homeless alcoholics proved that the desire to drink and memories of the implant surgery were eliminated by combining electroconvulsive therapy and a secretion of the drug propranolol directly following the memory.

He was waiting for her inside a hotel room in the Marriott Marquis at the San Diego Marina. She arrived a little bit after noon, and he had a feast of various culinary delights for them to enjoy. There were cumin-scented beef kebabs, roasted red pepper and walnut spread, garlic-oregano grilled pita bread, corn on the cob with mint-feta butter, Greek-style salad, and lemon ice cream sandwiches with blueberry swirl. Dr. Lawrence was munching on one of the kebabs when she knocked.

"Dr. Edelstein, I presume?" Dr. Lawrence repeated his jest. As a scientist, his sense of humor wasn't the most elaborately developed. She politely smiled at him and entered. He waved a hand toward the table which held the foods. "Please, enjoy. We'll get started in a moment."

The psychiatrist walked past him and sat down on the long green couch. There was a picture hanging on the wall of fishermen in a boat bringing in a huge marlin off the San Diego coast. "I'm sorry, Doctor, but I've been unable to eat ever since the detective was injured. I did receive a call from him, however, and he'll be back on the case in three days."

"Yes, and I hear the FBI will be accompanying him. We're going to have to be careful with our testing. Some of the procedures we use have not been approved by the government as yet. Frankly, that's one of the main reasons I wanted to work on the ashram." Dr. Lawrence wiped his greasy fingers on a cloth napkin and sat down next to her on the couch.

"I understand. My parents were the same way. In fact, speaking of The Singularity, my father knew Ray Kurzweil. They both said they thought it would happen in a private laboratory by scientists who took chances."

"Oh, yes. In fact, those terrorists may be on the right track when they pinpoint our efforts. I know of no other experiments that have made the advances we have. Your parents were very much part of our effort, and you should be proud."

"I was confused about their death for a while, but now that I've seen what you've done, I am proud. Can we get this testing over with? I want to be able to use this device for my own health." She smiled at Dr. Lawrence, and he knew it was time to enhance the process.

"By all means. I have my laptop over there," said Dr. Lawrence, pointing to the table near the door. "Could you please go into the back bedroom? I want to see how the signal functions from some distance. Once we put the platform through its paces, I'll turn the controls over to you."

Dr. Edelstein got up from the couch and walked into the back bedroom. When he heard the door close, Dr. Lawrence stood up and made his way over to the laptop. He sat down in the chair and hit the ctrl alt keys. Rachel's digital package came up on the screen. Lawrence clicked on the upload button.

After waiting ten minutes, Dr. Lawrence got up from the laptop and walked into the back of the hotel room. He turned the doorknob, exhaling slowly as he did so. He was beginning the fantasy of his adolescence, and he knew what he would see once he opened the door. If the package did what he expected, then Little Annie Fannie would be on the bed for him to enjoy.

The red lights glowed. She was lounging upon the silk top sheet in the nude, staring over at the revolving lava lamps that stood on the dresser like the Queen's Guard at Buckingham Palace. Her dark eyebrows rose as he walked toward the end of the bed, letting his gaze slowly move up her body starting at the feet. Her calves were a 3.0 on the erotic scale, but the back of her knees went up to 5.0. Up to her thighs, his calculations continued, inner thigh, 6.0, clitoris, 9.0, and labia majora (7.0) and minora (8.0), and his mouth began to water. Upward slowly, her navel (5.0), her left breast (5.0), her right breast (6.0), and then the surprising left ear at 10.0 and right ear at 9.0. He took off his Oxfords, his trousers, then his shirt, and he finally tossed his boxers and T-shirt on the pile of clothes next to the bed.

When Dr. Lawrence knelt next to her head on the bed, he slowly began to swirl the pink helmet of his member all around the pinna, or the outer cartilage of her left ear. She moaned. When he placed the tip of his erect penis inside her ear canal, she began to writhe, just the way Annie had on his laptop inside the Caltech dorm room.

In fact, she moaned and writhed so seductively her ear began to move against the bottom shaft of his penis, until he felt that urgent urge building at the base of his testicles. When she took hold of his penis, he couldn't hold back; he came all over her ear, the gobs of his semen dripping down the side of her head, from the top of her black hair down to the bottom of her earlobe.

Dr. Lawrence fell back on the bed exhausted, and cursed, "Shit! Fuck!" What kind of lover was he? The entire experiment was going to waste, and he was furious.

When she began to laugh, he became enraged. He forgot all about his experiment, as he was once more a shamed adolescent. He got up and quickly got dressed, but he began to calm down when he realized she wouldn't remember any of this anyway. He also knew that it was her ability to control her orgasms and eliminate the traumas of her past that made this device valuable to society.

After dressing, he stood at the bedroom door. He looked back at her, and gazed down at his cell phone. She should be receiving the erasing ECT and propranolol in 4 . . .3 . . . 2 . . . 1. He watched Dr. Edelstein's mouth grimace, her eyes wince, and she simultaneously let out a sharp yelp. Dr. Lawrence smiled, stepped out of the bedroom, and closed the door.

"Jewish whore!" he muttered under his breath.

Rachel

After the bombing inside Omshanti, I was expecting to become paralyzed with fear and nightmares. Instead, my brain reacted with a strange, soothing calmness that poured through my body like a silent stream of serenity. It was as if my body were being regulated by a system much stronger than the neurotic chaos which had ruled my life up to that moment. I could give only one answer as to why this should happen, and I was going to visit the person who had implanted that cure inside the amygdala portion of my brain.

Just before I left for the Marriott Marquis, Detective Schlotsky called me from the hospital. He had been out of surgery for only four hours. He'd had some skin grafts to repair the third-degree burns on his face. "I look like Leatherface in *The Texas Chainsaw Massacre*," he said. "But the good news is I'll be working along with the full resources of the FBI. They should be in touch with you shortly to put you under protection."

I told him that his burns should heal eventually, and leave no scar tissue, as medicine is doing wonders with skin grafts. I also said I was going to cooperate fully with the Feds.

"Don't go inside Omshanti until we can find out who's behind this." His voice was adamant.

"I don't think you should be going in there either," I told him.

"What Jew have you seen put on a suicide vest for the cause? I wear a *Chai* around my neck because it means life. I plan to stay in the land of the living as long as I can."

I told him I was happy to hear that and I cut the connection.

I was able to drive my Golf without taking any drug to calm my agoraphobia. When I got to the fourth floor of the hotel, room 416, I felt quite at ease. I was certainly ready to continue the further testing of my Serene Implant.

Dr. Joshua Lawrence had a nice spread of food for us, but I told him I was eager to get finished with the beta tests. Although I was calm, I told him my appetite had been affected by the recent bombing at the ashram. I also told him about Detective Schlotsky calling me from the hospital and that the FBI would soon be on the case with him.

Dr. Lawrence explained the dangers of having the Feds on the case and that he was doing some research that would not be approved by the government. I told him my parents also worked for Guru Sharma because they believed The Singularity was going to happen in a private laboratory that wasn't afraid to take chances.

He told me to go into the back bedroom because he wanted to see how the WiFi worked at some distance. He also said he was going to turn the controls over to me once the test was completed. When I was inside the bedroom, I sat down on the end of the mattress with my clothes on. I noticed there were several lava lamp lights on the dresser that emitted a red glow. Quite frankly, it felt like I was inside a prostitute's lair.

The next few moments I waited. When the SLIC was activated, I had a rush of joy fill my consciousness that can only be approximated in words. It was like a child's exhilaration on her birthday or a young lover's passion upon seeing the person of their dreams returning after many months. I could see flowing colors streaming through the air, and music became a vibration at every sensitive part of my body. It was as if my entire being had been transformed into a love receptor that could divine any potent desire within my direct circle of radiating light.

I slowly took off my clothes to the rhythm of the music and the pulsing red glow of the lava lights. I knew another passionate being would be walking through that door, but I was not aware, nor did I care, who he or she was. I was simply waiting in order to awaken to a different life other than my own and to rejoice at the inner knowledge that I knew was going to happen.

When he entered the bedroom, I could envision something I had never before experienced. This person who entered did have a singular identity, but he was also connected to every second of his existence, and these seconds were laid out evenly in the air before my eyes like a visual display. What made this a completely unique ability was the fact that I could intuit those moments in his life when he had been affected by sexual trauma. It was as if my abilities as a psychoanalyst had been enhanced beyond my wildest dreams.

He stands in the shower with other, much older males. He is the genius in school, having to compete biologically with men. He tried to lather his hairless penis and crotch with soap to hide his youth. If he can make it bigger, maybe they won't notice. They turn and laugh, and one of them walks over and flicks his thumb and forefinger at the tip of his penis. He screams.

Alone inside his dorm room, he moves his hand up and down the shaft of his penis. On the laptop screen is a female who is licking and sucking on the ball sack of a male with a very large penis. She is beneath him, and as she begins to fondle her own vagina, he comes all over the paper tissue he holds beneath his erection. Again, a roommate enters just as he comes, and laughs at him. Later, on the Caltech campus, beneath an oak tree, three older students pull down his pants and chant, 'Little Annie Fannie's Weenie Boy! Little Annie Fannie's Weenie Boy!'

These visions kept repeating before me until the man began to talk. He seemed to be speaking about some numerical scale of evaluation, as his eyes pored over my body. Was he grading me? Did he feel so inferior that he needed to assign some system of grading my body?

When his small erect penis touched my ear, however, I couldn't help but squirm and moan. This was one of my special passion points, and yet the pictures of his many humiliations still continued to move past my inner vision like a counter-balance to this display of ridiculous sexual energy.

She tells him she is Jewish and just wants to make some extra money to pay for acting school. When she disrobes in front of him, he gets hard, and she tells him she'll give him a blow job for twenty, and he can copulate with her for fifty. He says he wants to copulate, but when he gets on top of her, he pushes his face on hers. She says she cannot kiss any client. She says she only kisses her true lover. His face turns beet red, and he stands at the side of the bed, his pecker already beginning to wither. 'You Jewish whore! How dare you rebuff me!'

When he ejaculated on my ear, I was seeing this fragment from his life, and I began to laugh.

Visibly infuriated, he got up from the bed, quickly dressed, and stood at the door. He was counting, and then I felt a sharp, piercing pain in the front of my forehead. When he left the room, he was smiling. Although I felt pain, I could still remember every moment that had taken place.

CHAPTER THIRTEEN: THE SLEUTHING BEGINS

Rachel

The person I wanted to talk to first about what happened inside the Marriott was Jacob Stein. Not only was he a fellow traveler, he was also a psychoanalyst. He was much more technologically proficient than I am, so he could help me understand what might have happened to my brain.

I texted him, and he said he would cancel two patients to meet with me at his office at the UCSD Medical Center in Hillcrest. As I walked out to my Golf, I noticed that my emotional trauma vision kicked into action only when I was closer than five feet away from another human. Once the person got within close range, I began to see the moments in that person's history laid out in the air before me like digital video inside editing software. All I needed to do to watch and listen to the event was concentrate on the moment, and it began to play out. To move between the various moments, I just blinked my eyes, and the next trauma would come into view.

Jacob hugged me when I entered his office. "Rachel, I'm so happy you came! Please, sit down and tell me what's been happening."

I sat down on his patient's couch and turned to face him. As his traumatic history came into view, I held myself back. I suddenly realized that having this kind of information was giving me a lot of power over another person. When I would hypnotize or even use drugs, I was never certain I would get a clear picture of what might have actually happened in my patient's life to affect the present. In fact, as Freud knew, most of the worst neuroses came about because the patient would confuse the actual event with something he believed he remembered. This completely imaginary event was, most often, much worse than the actual event had been.

With my new ability to see, in real time, the brain's recording of the event—if that's what I was seeing—there could be no confusing interpretation getting in the way of the actual trauma. As they say in computer terms, this was "what you see is what you get."

"I don't know where to begin, Jacob. I assume you know about the three murders of Jews and the recent explosion at the Omshanti commune?" He nodded, so I continued.

"Detective Howard Schlotsky was injured in that explosion, and he's also a Jew, and then there was the anti-Semitic declaration inside the canister. They're threatening to kill more Jews and to go higher up in the chain of command because they say The Singularity can't work unless the world is purged of Jews."

"Does it never end? And then there's the irony that the guy who invented the concept of The Singularity is a Jew. I assume the FBI will be in on this case now that they've admitted wanting to kill Jews. That's a good thing, no?"

"Yes, I suppose. Listen, Jacob. I want to tell you what I've come up with. I have some of my own theories about who might have committed these murders. Also, I seem to have been given a new mental ability that came about after I agreed to be a human beta tester of a brain implant."

"What the hell! You let somebody operate on your brain?" Jacob sat forward and took my hands in his. "Who did this to you?"

"As you know, I was trying to find a way to treat my psychoses. My parents lost their lives from the first implants back in 1992, and so I was shown all the progress that has been made since then by this Caltech genius, Dr. Joshua Lawrence. It was truly amazing how far they've come, Jacob, so I agreed to become the Serene's first beta tester."

"None of this is approved by the government. How can you risk your life like this?"

"Let me explain. I don't think what happened to me was what Dr. Lawrence had planned. I think he was just trying to get his rocks off at my expense, but I don't think he was able to erase my memory of the event—if that was what he was trying to do. Instead of becoming a willing sex machine who responds vigorously to every one of his programmed titillations of my body, I became kind of a super-psychoanalyst. That's why I wanted to talk to you first before I involve the police."

"Super-psychoanalyst? You mean, like the Marvel comics? A superpower?"

"Not exactly. No x-ray vision or flying. What I can do is see others in a very special way. When I am five feet away from a person, or closer, a strange display appears in front of my vision. I am able to watch memory recordings of every sexually traumatizing event in that person's life. They appear in the air like holograms. All I have to do is blink my eyes, and I can go on to the next event. I saw three of Dr. Lawrence's traumas while he was testing me at the Marriott Marquis."

"Where did they place this implant?"

"It was a tiny sensor, the width of a human hair. They inserted it inside the amygdala, within the medial temporal lobe."

"That could explain why you're getting these signals, but are you certain they're not your own traumas you're seeing? Declarative and episodic memories are stored in the medial temporal region, but this is your brain, not another person's brain."

"I saw Dr. Lawrence as a boy in college in these mind videos. None of these experiences was from my life."

"Well, I have been reading about a group that can now convert brain waves and memories into pictures. Maybe your brain was converted into some kind of receiver of specific events that are transmitted from the person's medial temporal lobe into your receiver, where the electronic signals get decrypted into visual images. In your case, I suppose, your implant became a receiver and converter of traumatic events in others. When they get close enough to your receiver, you're able to pick up these signals and they're then decrypted into visual images."

"Do you think Dr. Lawrence knew this would happen?" From the way he behaved and the way he looked at me when I felt the shock just before he left the room, I couldn't believe Lawrence knew what happened inside my brain.

"I can't say. However, if he were going to treat your sexual traumas, I can't believe he meant for you to be able to read other people's minds, do you? I would think he'd want to condition your subconscious to respond the way he wanted you to. A psychologist at The Academic College of Tel-Aviv Yaffo in Israel says that the human brain can be hacked just the way a computer can be hacked. They use odor to crack the subconscious brain to respond in a certain way. It seems smell is the only sense that can bypass the thalamus and affect the unconscious. Did you smell any odors when they did the implant?"

"No. Now let me tell you about what I've deduced from the events. Dr. Lawrence called me a Jewish whore, and this would make me believe he's anti-Semitic. He also has the technical genius to create the canister bomb that could not be registered on the bomb-sniffing robot. I also think he believed he was erasing my memory during my beta test. I felt a tremendous shock in my forehead, and I saw him smile before he left the room. That would lead me to believe he could be behind this entire plot to murder Jews. Of course, Guru Sharma may also be giving him the instructions, but I tend to believe Lawrence is acting on his own."

"Yes, I can understand your logic, Rachel. However, you're now going to have the FBI and probably the NSA swarming all over Omshanti like locusts. Don't you think it's better to leave the investigating up to them right now?"

"I guess you're right. But I still want to try out my new ability to see if I can turn up more information. Would you like to join me in a bit of psychological sleuthing?"

"So, you're not going to tell the authorities about what you can do?"

"No, why should I? They would just put me under a microscope and probably quarantine me. I don't need to be probed like an alien."

"All right, Rachel. I'll go with you. I'll be your Dr. Watson." Jacob stood up and gave me another hug. "What do you see, pray tell, about me? I hope you don't watch the time my cousin Sarah and I played doctor in my uncle's office."

Detective Schlotsky was calling me, so I picked up.

"Rachel, there's been another murder. This time, it's not a Jew. The FBI said they found Dr. Joshua Lawrence's body inside his genetics lab."

Part of me was relieved to hear this news, but another part of me was quite frightened. Was I like Frankenstein's monster unleashed upon the world? What exactly did Lawrence put inside my brain to cause all of these visions? Maybe I was next on the list to die. Could my brain explode like that canister did? If Dr. Lawrence wasn't the killer, then who was it?

PART THREE: BONE OF MY BONES, FLESH OF MY FLESH

SERENE

CHAPTER FOURTEEN: THE FEDS

Guru

When he saw the single file of ten plain black Chryslers enter Omshanti, one after the other, Guru Bhagwan Sharma realized he was being taken over by a government he had never really trusted. To him, they represented the authority to shut down any group or religious organization they believed posed a threat to the status quo. The three FBI agents that questioned him that day were much different than the local police detective named Schlotsky.

They all wore the same matching black suits, and they never removed the sunglasses they had on, even when they were seated across from him inside his temple office. Their rigid, authoritarian manners contrasted sharply with the multi-colored paintings of Hindu Gods and Goddesses covering his walls. They each took turns asking him questions, with the first one, the shortest, speaking in a deep bass, monotone voice.

"Mr. Sharma, where were you when your colleague, Dr. Lawrence, was knifed to death?"

"I was supervising the Shiva and Shakti dance practice in our dining hall. One of Dr. Lawrence's lab assistants, Monica, came running into the room screaming the news."

"Have you had any altercations or disagreements with Dr. Lawrence?"

"Nothing that would warrant such a horrible act. He was my chief scientist and the head of research and development. In fact, I know of nobody who would want to harm Dr. Lawrence." The Guru watched as the next agent took the center seat in this game of musical chairs.

"Again, we could find no traces of DNA other than the victim's. I noticed you have robots all over the campus here. Do they go into labs or other rooms to clean?"

"Yes, they routinely go inside all of the buildings to clean but only at eight hour intervals. There was no cleaning scheduled until midnight."

The last of the agents, a thin man with red hair, took the inquisitive hot seat. "We looked at the digital camera recording for that time in the genetics lab, and we found ten minutes were edited out of the memory. Who is responsible for keeping your security camera records?"

79

"Dr. Lawrence ultimately signs off on all the security recordings of Omshanti. He delegates the retrieval of the camera recordings each day to different members of our research laboratory staff. However, this is done every eight hours, the same time that the robot cleaning is done. There is no way of tracing the record in this instance because somebody obviously edited the digital recording before the regularly scheduled time."

"I suppose when it comes to trust, you may want to give more assignments to your robot staff," the agent smiled, but the short fellow, most likely his superior, cleared his throat. "That's enough, Barstow. Mr. Sharma, thank you for your information. You've been helpful. In the next few days, we will be searching and questioning quite a bit around here. You need to suspend your regular activities until our crime scene investigation is completed. In addition, we can't allow anybody to leave the compound unless we escort them."

"We will cooperate, sir. This is obviously a great shock to our group, and we certainly want to find out who did this as much as you want to bring the guilty party to justice."

"One more thing. We need to have your police unit turn over all of their weapons to us. Until this crime scene is secured, everyone is a possible suspect."

"I completely understand. I'll have it done immediately." The Guru stood up behind his desk and put his palms together to bow. "Namaste."

The FBI agents nodded to the Guru and filed out of the office behind him.

Rachel

"Why do you have to concern yourself with the FBI? If we're going to become Holmes and Watson, then why don't we act like them?" Dr. Jacob Stein, who had quite a few more sexual traumas in his history than he imagined, was making some good sense. When Jacob suggested we become independent investigators, I was quickly warming to the idea.

I called Detective Schlotsky, who was our inside contact, and he thought it was actually a good idea as well. "No matter how much brain power these folks claim to have, I'm certain they don't have two psychiatrists who know as much as you two do about what goes on inside religious groups. Plus, you're also Jews, and the anti-Semitic nature of these crimes are quite apparent to them. Let me talk to Special Agent Val Ryan. He's the head honcho on this case. I'm sure he'll need to get you both cleared for security, but I don't see why he won't let you help us on these cases. He wants to question you anyway, so ask for him when you get here."

As we drove out to San Marcos to meet with Special Agent Ryan, Jacob told me how worried he had been about me. When he heard on the news about the explosion, he wanted to call me, but he was afraid I no longer wanted to see him on a personal basis. I admitted that my mental health at the time caused me to do some things I was now regretting, but now that I had this new ability, I needed somebody who could help me understand what I was seeing and how it can be of use.

"Now that Dr. Lawrence has been murdered, how does it change your ideas about who the murderer might be?" Jacob asked.

"I really don't know. I suppose if we can find some evidence that Guru Sharma was behind the murder, then he would be the likely suspect. Or, perhaps there's another person within the research component who would stand to be promoted into Lawrence's job. I haven't really probed into the hierarchy at Omshanti, so I can't say right now. I think the FBI can help us out on that score."

There were police cars all over the compound. If the murderer were a member of Omshanti, then this would be the time to be vigilant. I had my suspicions that the murderer was a technologist. There was no evidence of DNA at the crime scenes, so they must have been able to clean everything down to the microscopic level. They also had to be able to travel from Israel back to California without raising any suspicion. That would eliminate anybody on the terrorist watch lists.

We were told by an FBI agent at the front gate that Special Agent Ryan was questioning Omshanti members. He was using Guru Sharma's office to do so, so we headed over there. The agent told us he was texting the special agent about our arrival, and we should be able to go right in.

Special Agent Val Ryan was a twenty-year vet with silver hair, no sunglasses, and a buff body that looked very good on a fifty-plus-year-old. His smile was generous and not pasted on, and his gray eyes were deep-set into a tanned and wrinkled face. He was seated behind the Guru's desk like he was the Swami, and Detective Schlotsky, fresh from the hospital, was seated to his right. The grafts on Schlotsky's face were hardly visible except for some red puffiness on the borders. They were talking when we entered, and they both turned to face us as we sat down in two government-issue gray metal folding chairs.

I could see the traumatic histories of all three men from my position, and I was tempted to explore them out of curiosity, but I knew it was irrelevant to the task at hand. The only man I was there to investigate was Bhagwan Sharma. While Ryan was questioning Sharma, I was going to be watching the sexual traumas of my guru. But I first had to introduce my dear Watson to the FBI.

"Special Agent Ryan, this is Dr. Jacob Stein. He is also a psychoanalyst, and we would like to join your team to perhaps assist you in your search for the perpetrators. We both believe the suspect or suspects are probably technologists who are highly educated. In fact, until Dr. Lawrence was murdered, I believed he was the most suspicious."

"You don't say. That's quite interesting, Dr. Edelstein. He was on our list of important suspects, but what do you know that gave him a special motive?"

"As you probably know, I was working with Dr. Lawrence on a new device he was testing in his lab. Since the bombing, Jews were not allowed on these premises, so we took our experiment off-site to the Marriott Marquis at the Marina. When the experiment didn't work out the way Dr. Lawrence wanted it to, he called me a Jewish whore. I have reason to believe he also thought I would not be able to remember what he had done to me, but I wanted to check with you about that. If he were anti-Semitic, then I would assume this makes him a prime suspect. He was certainly a well-qualified technologist, and the device he was working on, the Serene Libido Implant Controller, could have given him a great resource to sell to the private sector or even to the government."

"Funny you should bring up the SLIC. I just got through questioning Dr. Monica Farley. She was Dr. Lawrence's assistant on this and other projects."

"Yes, she was the one who prepared me for the implant," I interrupted.

"She told me that they had recently tested the memory erasure component with a homeless person. It worked. Dr. Farley also told me she was working closely with him on the robotics project. She said the creation of the androids that were your parents was the major accomplishment. Even though she is in line to take over Dr. Lawrence's job, it was hardly a motive to kill him. Guru Bhagwan Sharma has financial control over all of the projects created in the labs. Therefore, he would be the one to benefit from any commercial patent or sales."

"So, you're basically back to square one," said Jacob. "What about The Singularity component that Rachel says was mentioned in the directive inside the orange bomb? Are any of the projects pursuing this goal of self-awareness?"

As Jacob was saying this, I couldn't help but see my own powers of visualizing their sexual histories right there in the same room. Could I have been Lawrence's path to this Singularity? It was an interesting question, but I knew it would be too dangerous to tell the authorities about it. Now that Lawrence was dead, I also became a prime motive in this horrendous plot. Would he create The Singularity inside me, a Jewish whore? Maybe he became a murder target because his ironic sense of humor wasn't so funny to the real murderers. As a result, as the logic goes, these murderers would also want to get rid of me to purge the world for the real awakening to follow.

CHAPTER FIFTEEN: INVESTIGATING THE GURU

Guru

The murder of Dr. Joshua Lawrence created the worst public relations problem in the history of the Omshanti ashram. Guru Bhagwan Sharma knew that the good work being done in his science labs was secret, so all the public knew was that a murder had been committed inside his commune and that it was tied to an international case against Jews. Feature stories were done on television and in the press about the four murders and about how the FBI had closed down the ashram and all the businesses it owned in San Marcos.

Guru Sharma also had to respond directly to the accusations that were coming out about his relations with underage girls. Five previous women who had been chosen as his brides of passion came out with personal stories concerning his love chamber. Even though this practice was closed down in 1992, after Rachel Edelstein left the commune, it was a bad mark on the Guru's record. The press discovered that the Guru had first begun this molestation of girls in India, and he then continued the practice when he moved to California.

Special Agent Ryan interviewed the Guru for four hours. Sharma found it strange that Rachel Edelstein and her friend, Dr. Jacob Stein, were also present during the questioning. He was told that the two psychiatrists were assisting in the case and had been cleared for security.

Guru Sharma gave the complete history of his ashram and its philosophy, including the goal of preparing the Milky Way Galaxy for the convergence with his native galaxy, Andromeda. The agent seemed to be especially interested when Guru told him about the practice of Tantra and sexual joining of members in order to achieve an enlightened consciousness. Guru explained the goal of their union of masculine and feminine, and he pointed out that the maleness and femaleness were only symbolic and that the union can also be male with male and female with female.

"The purpose of Tantric practice is recognizing our own Divine nature, the Divine nature of our partner and everything around us simply as a never-ending sacred dance between the two principles of the universe: Shiva—masculine stillness, ultimate consciousness—and

Shakti—feminine energy, manifestation on all levels. This is the core of Love in the Tantric sense. In Tantra we embrace the body with all its desires, and we embark on a path to reprogram ourselves through the power of the Sacred Union of Shiva and Shakti. This sexual union is an inevitable part of the process in order to incorporate this new perspective on reality. As often misinterpreted in the West, Tantra is not only about increasing our libido or our levels of pleasure and satisfaction, and the goal is not to become the best lover in the Universe. All these are only the side effects."

"What do you make of the murder of Sergeant Seth Berman? The body had a desecrated Star of David, and he had ejaculated just before his throat was cut. We saw that the Maithuna is a Tantric symbol that looks just like the Jewish Star of David. Could there be a connection between your practitioners and the belief that Jews are defaming the Maithuna?" Dr. Stein, the person who studied symbols in his profession, was asking this.

"Yes, the Maithuna symbol is a hexagon, but there are other practices that use this image. I don't believe it necessarily means a Tantric devotee would do this," said Guru Sharma.

"If you believe you're from a planet in another galaxy, then how can you be so certain about what is practiced on this one?" Special Agent Ryan was being sarcastic. The Guru ignored his comment.

"Also, what about your science goals? The murdered Dr. Lawrence believed he was on the verge of creating The Singularity. Does his goal correlate with your so-called sexually spiritual practices?" Ryan leaned forward. He asked this question at almost the three-hour mark of the interview, and the Guru was the only one who seemed calm. Rachel was twisting and turning in her chair.

"We always met to make certain our goals were convergent. After all, the ultimate goal of Omshanti is the convergence of two galactic identities. Tantra believes men and women must repair the torn shreds of their identities by joining together in sexual union. Dr. Lawrence explained to me that The Singularity also had a goal of unifying the evolution of mankind so that only the positive attributes of life would be developed and improved upon," said the Guru.

"How can you stop evil acts? Isn't selfishness and greed part of human nature?" Rachel asked.

"According to Dr. Lawrence, human nature, as you call it, will be transformed forever. The Singularity will usher in a future period during which the pace of technological change will be so rapid, its impact so deep, that human life will be irreversibly transformed. Although neither utopian nor dystopian, this epoch will transform the concepts that we rely on to give meaning to our lives, from our business models to the cycle of human life, including death itself."

The meeting ended, and the Guru gave his guests Namaste, and left to go on his weekly drive through the compound. Even though the activities were not going on, his devotees still expected to see their master.

Rachel

I now understood what the physicists discuss when they talk about reality being divided into parallel universes. As we visited Guru Sharma inside his temple office, what I saw within that room as I sat no more than five feet from these men was a universe filled with virtual reality. In front of each man there was the same display: a long row of framed images that represented each sexually traumatic moment in that man's life. I could see movement inside each frame that showed me it was a living memory.

The possibilities of helping victims of post-traumatic stress disorder were also there. In the United States Armed Forces, there are about twenty-two suicides each day related to PTSD issues. If I could assist these people by using my new ability, then lives could be saved. First, however, I needed to see if this technical phenomena, started by my parents, was based on truth and not upon some hallucinatory figment of my imagination. What better way to prove it than to investigate these murders by using my amplified analytical powers?

Physicists also say that time and space are one and the same, so what I was seeing was the past, which never actually disappears. Actually, why should it? It affects our every waking moment in that my job as a psychiatrist is to probe those past experiences and clear out the misinformation created by a brain that does not have the crystal-clear access to the event that I was now experiencing. Was it some malfunction in my implant that was causing my new inner visual clarity?

Perhaps each of us is genetically programmed with wired-in abilities that can be super-charged by the experience of having an implant like the SLIC? Maybe when Dr. Lawrence thought he was able to control the implant by computer, it was the individual's brain that actually took over the process and controlled how the brain would produce the results in the uniquely gifted way it had for me. I was hoping I could find out if it were this mistake that may have resulted in Dr. Lawrence's murder.

Whatever had actually happened, I believed I could now use my unique gift to explore Bhagwan Sharma's sexual history. As I listened to Special Agent Ryan quiz the Guru, I looked at the first traumatic memory that hovered in front of his body like an LCD screen. I could see the actors in this drama, and I could also hear the Guru's interior monologue. It was truly an omniscient viewpoint. The next memory could be viewed by blinking my eyes.

I have safely continued the sacred ritual. They bring each bride of passion to me at the monthly full moon. Each one is without identification of any kind. As a homeless child, society no longer wants her. Only I will make her a blazing star in the Cosmos. When she conjoins with me, the Andromeda planets will move closer to the great Convergence.

Who is this that dares enter my chamber before the ritual? Dr. Lawrence looks angry. He says he wants to take these girls to sell on the sex tourism market. Without this income, his scientific research will not be able to be continued.

I tell him that once these young women become my brides they are protected by the universal love. They cannot be used for lust, especially lust that makes a profit. He screams at me, and I am trying to calm him down. He tells me, 'How do you think you've been able to keep the ashram running all these years? The Singularity must not be polluted with Zionists. The biggest banks, including the Federal Reserve, are enslaving the world to debt-based currencies all run by Zionist Jews: Rothschild's of London and Berlin, Lazard Brothers of Paris, Israel Moses Seaf of Italy, Kuhn, Loeb and Company of Germany and New York, Warburg and Company of Germany, Lehman Brothers of New York, Goldman Sachs of New York, Rockefeller Brothers of New York, and many more. The biggest and most influential lobby in

America is AIPAC, the American Israel Public Affairs Committee, and the majority of Congress has long been bought out by Israeli interests.'

I have never heard such anti-Semitic talk coming from Dr. Lawrence. I try to discover how he would believe such nonsense, but he screams again, 'The media is also controlled by Jews, so when the world needs to know the truth about what's happening in the Middle East, information becomes polluted with their propaganda. You stupid fool! I have been eliminating these Jews in your honor. When your two Jews tried to stop me from selling the homeless girls and boys, I had to kill them. When the Convergence takes place, The Singularity will be in place, and the necessary purity will also be instated. If you speak one word about this, you will also be eliminated. Just as you have your followers around the world, so do I have my own devotees. However, my followers are willing to kill to purify the world, while you think you can fuck your way to paradise!'

I can hear Special Agent Ryan ask the Guru about the goals of Tantra and The Singularity. Guru sounds like there is no dark side to either philosophy. From what I have learned by his trauma, each philosophy was on a deadly collision course. "How can you stop evil acts? Isn't selfishness and greed part of human nature?" I asked.

When they continued the questioning, I perused some of the other traumas in the Guru's list, but none was about the murders. He had a few concerned with masturbation and one about being tempted by the variety of women in the ashram.

Now I knew with certainty who had murdered my parents and the other Jews. But who killed Dr. Lawrence? The logical person to suspect would be Guru Sharma, but although I believe he was terrified by what Lawrence and his followers represented, I don't think he could commit murder. I did remember that in Israel, when a terrorist who murders innocent civilians is captured, the authorities know that torturing the prisoner will do nothing to get information out of him. Instead, they go after his or her relatives. Maybe I could find out more about Dr. Lawrence's relatives or close associates.

The FBI would never believe evidence based on my super-analytical ability to read the minds of others. I might as well be reading tea leaves. No, unless I got some substantiated proof that Dr. Lawrence killed those people, the hunt would continue. The danger would intensify now that their leader was out of the picture. Armed with the advanced technology that Lawrence had developed in his labs, perfect murders could soon be popping up like poisonous mushrooms in a dark forest. This was not Paradise on Earth. This was Hell on Earth.

I decided that my only hope to bring down this group of terrorists was to approach Guru Sharma directly and tell him what I know. If he was truly a spiritual man, then I believed he would help me. If he had aligned himself with these evil forces, then he would also have to be brought to justice.

CHAPTER SIXTEEN: ANOTHER CONVERGENCE

Rachel

When I told Jacob what I had seen and heard about Guru Sharma's confrontation with Dr. Lawrence, he agreed that we needed to go directly to Sharma. This was our only hope at getting the evidence needed to close these cases and track down the perpetrators.

"I think if Sharma tells the FBI about what Dr. Lawrence was doing, they can certainly discover proof on their own to prove his guilt. There must be a paper or digital trail left by the culprits who were making these deals." Jacob was playing a very good Dr. Watson, and he was even accepting my supernatural sleuthing abilities. Holmes was a drugged-out genius with a photographic memory, and I was drug-prescribing shrink with mind-reading sex radar. I needed Jacob to keep me focused.

Bhagwan Sharma was not surprised when he heard that I had seen his confrontation with Dr. Lawrence by using an ability that was given to me after a brain implant. In fact, he was going to tell the authorities that Lawrence had committed those murders, but he was afraid for his own life.

"I'm so happy you have come to give me the courage to do this. Rachel, your parents were good scientists and human beings. They believed the convergence would take place, and they even approved of my union with the brides of passion. I had their approval to join with you, even though the law said it was not permitted. I am a gentle man who only wants peace for the world. You do believe me, don't you?"

Guru's penetrating brown eyes could still work their magic on me, even though my new perspective gave me a much loftier view of the human dilemma. Compared to the evil acts Dr. Lawrence and his followers were committing, Sharma's bride of passion ritual was relatively harmless.

"Yes, now that I see how you meant no physical or mental harm to me or to the other girls, I respect your belief, even though I still don't agree with it. Sergeant Seth Berman, who was the first murder victim, tried to tell me my parents were selling homeless girls and boys to the tourist sex trade. When you found out they were doing this, Sid and Rose supposedly committed suicide from shame. Now we know it was Dr. Lawrence who did all of this. If you go to Special Agent Ryan and tell him all that you know, I'm certain he won't prosecute you for rape. We must track down these followers of Lawrence before they can commit any more crimes."

"Who would have the records we're looking for?" Jacob asked.

"Dr. Farley kept all the financial records of the Research and Development end of things. I was issued monthly reports, but I would assume the records you're looking for were kept by Farley."

"That makes total sense. We'll go over to see her right now. In which building does she live?" I was anxious to get over there. My newly-acquired powerful intuition told me things were going to start moving very fast, and we needed to act quickly.

"Her apartment is room 212 inside the Ion Proton Genetics Lab," Sharma said. "May the Lord Vishnu protect you."

Dr. Monica Farley was a graduate of MIT, and she was born in Fall River, Massachusetts to two college professors. I established an instant rapport with her, even though two of her sexual traumas had to do with bestiality with two large dogs she had as pets. I am fairly open-minded when it comes to the whole LBGTQ community, but I draw the line at animals.

"Yes, I have the complete record of transactions we've made. What exactly are you looking for?" She was a tall and thin woman in her forties, with the dark, fish-eyed look of the Morticia character on that old TV horror comedy, *The Addams Family*.

"Anything that might show transactions between foreign hotels or tourist locations," I said.

"Dr. Lawrence never kept me apprised on what exactly he was purchasing. Unless it had a supply code, I really didn't know what it might be. Do they think they know who might have killed him?" Her voice was matter-of-fact, so I supposed there wasn't any really close relationship between the two.

Dr. Farley searched through the database on her laptop. Finally, she stopped, and printed out ten pages of spreadsheets. She handed them to me with a smile playing on her thin lips. "There were over two hundred payments over the years to hotels and spas around the world. Do you know what it might concern?"

"I'm afraid we can't tell you yet, but you might have just cracked our murder case wide open. I thank you, Doctor," I said, and we left.

After we explained what Guru Sharma told us about the tourist sex trafficking of Omshanti's young homeless, the FBI was able to quickly track down the financial deals being made between Dr. Lawrence and the hotels and other organizations in other countries. They, in fact, had a complete record of most of the major players in this multi-billion-dollar industry.

Things happened pretty quickly after that. The money transfers to the sex tourist spots were verified, and Lawrence was indeed making quite a profit from the transfer of his homeless population to these traffickers.

"From August of 1996, to September of this year, he turned a profit of over eight million dollars. Lawrence had a secret wire transfer between the traffickers, so his records only showed his payments out for business visits to other countries. In fact, they were locations of the biggest tourist spots for the sex tourism racket. One of our cybercrime guys was able to locate the bank account, so now we have evidence." Special Agent Ryan spread out the paperwork on the table inside Guru Sharma's office.

"Do you think you have enough to close these cases?" I asked.

"I think so. Even though there was no DNA evidence at any of the crime scenes, we can speculate that Dr. Lawrence could have easily used one of his handy robots to clean up the area after the murder was committed."

"What about the murder of Dr. Lawrence? I assume you no longer suspect me," said Guru Sharma.

"No, we don't suspect you. You had no reason to kill him other than if you were collecting the money from the sex trafficking business. We know now you weren't aware of it. In fact, we have a major lead that makes us suspect one of the sex traffickers. You see, Dr. Lawrence also enjoyed himself some action with the prostitutes at these establishments. Miguel Monterrey, a known cartel member and owner of the Last Chance Ranchero in Cancun, was after Lawrence to pay a big debt that was owed. Lawrence promised Monterrey a shipment of ten homeless, and he never delivered. We think the cartel probably put the hit on the doctor."

"The result is the Feds will be closing up shop tomorrow. I'll also be leaving, but we both want you to stay on our Rolodex," said Detective Howard Schlotsky. "We like the way you track down leads."

"I haven't heard the word 'Rolodex' used for fifteen years," said Jacob. "I knew the police weren't getting funded properly, but hey, Rolodexes? This isn't the Veterans Administration."

The men laughed. Only Guru and I didn't get the reference. I thought a Rolodex was a new app, and Guru probably thought it was some kind of mental telepathy.

Ocean Beach . . . one week later

I kept having a strange dream, so I thought I'd call my personal dream analyst, Dr. Stein. It wasn't the usual dream about being there when my Masada brethren committed suicide to escape the clutches of the Romans in 73 CE, but it was close.

"In this dream, I'm back in my unit with the IDF. We hear the sirens going off all over, so we assume Hamas in Gaza or Hezbollah in Lebanon are firing rockets at the homeland again. Instead, we hear over the loudspeakers the voice of Bibi himself, Prime Minister Akiva Fleischman. He tells us that he's the long-awaited Messiah, and that he must take action to protect us against an imminent invasion. We don't know what kind of action he's talking about, but we all wait, shaking in our collective boots for something to go down. That's when we see doors in the ground opening up to reveal stairs. Up these stairs come thousands upon thousands of warrior robots. As these robots reach the surface of the earth, they begin walking toward us, as we are assembled in lines awaiting orders. One by one, each robot moves to each soldier in uniform and stands beside him or her. Bibi's voice again comes out loudly over the speakers. 'You have now been relieved of duty, by order of the Israeli Defense Forces!' As soon as he speaks those words, all of us flesh-and-blood soldiers begin to dissolve, first our feet, then upward, until only our faces are there.

Simultaneous bolts of lightning strike all of our faces, and we're gone—poof! And the machines take over."

There's a long wait on the other end. Finally, I hear Jacob clear his throat. "The Singularity been on your mind lately?" he said.

"Yes! Why didn't I think of that? All of this implant business and my visions. Maybe I should get this damned implant taken out of me." I was scared.

"No, I think not. Look at it as a freak of circumstance, Rachel. If Lawrence hadn't operated on you, these cases would have never been solved. Who knows how many more Jews might have been murdered? Besides, I couldn't be your Watson, Mister Holmes."

I heard the buzz of call waiting. "Excuse me, Jacob. I need to take this other call."

"Sure."

"Rachel, you must come at once. Your parents are missing!" It was Guru Sharma.

At first, I thought I was caught in a time warp. Then I remembered the robots created with the image and minds of Sid and Rose. "Missing? What do you mean? I thought they were programmed to do only certain tasks. How can that happen?"

"I thought they were stable as well. Something must have changed in their CPU circuitry. Do you have any ideas about where they might have gone? We don't know the first place to look."

Strangely, my new dream came back to me. "It might be a long shot, but when they were alive, they always talked about going to Israel. They never made it there. It wasn't a religion thing, mind you, they just wanted to see all the new science that was happening over there."

"We don't have any other possibilities; so would you mind coming over? We already called Detective Schlotsky, and he's coming over also. How soon can you get here?"

"Dr. Stein and I will be there in about one-half hour. I'm going to check online for El Al prices to the Holy Land, just in case," I said, and I switched to Jacob's connection. "Hey, Jacob, guess what? My parental robots have flown the coop. The only place I could think of where they might have gone is to Israel. They never got to go. We need to meet the Guru in thirty minutes. Can I swing by and get you?"

"No, I'll get you. We can get there in fifteen minutes in my Porsche."

"Okay, but drive carefully."

CHAPTER SEVENTEEN: TEL AVIV

Rachel

There were three plainclothes Mossad agents to greet us as soon as we walked down the passageway into the airport terminal. Even though I had resigned my IDF commission many years before, they addressed me as "Captain Edelstein." They wore no suit and tie; instead, they looked like tourists on holiday in the Mediterranean. Dark, scruffy beards, loud tropical shirts and cool cotton slacks with loafers. As Californians, they made Jacob and me feel right at home.

The Mossad see themselves as sabras. Historically, the sabra had to ignore his personal life. He had to dedicate his life to the security needs of the majority. These young zealous sabras were once the core of the paramilitary organizations such as the "Palmach" (Hagana), the "Irgun" and the "Lehi" (Stern group). They were the ones who volunteered to serve in the Jewish Brigade in 1944 in order to fight against the Nazis. They were also the ones who became the secret assassins against radical Islamists and other enemies of the State of Israel.

Mossad Agent Avi Morgenstern was the commanding officer we met once we were whisked downtown to their offices in Tel Aviv. He reported directly to the Director, Yossi Nusbaum, who in turn reported directly to Prime Minister Fleischman. He was a tall man who did wear a suit, but it was a white, seersucker variety, rather like that of a plantation owner in the Deep South. He was a dark-complexioned Yemenite, with a long scar that ran from his forehead to the bottom of his chin. He had a thick, Hebrew accent, and as he pointed for us to sit in the provided chairs in his office, he at first spoke in Hebrew.

"Do you both speak Hebrew?"

"No, Jacob is a California surfer Jew who never learned much Hebrew. He's also a clinical psychoanalyst," I said.

"Good. I trust you learned enough to Bar Mitzvah," Avi said, in halting English, almost bringing himself to smile, but not quite.

"No, I'm afraid my folks weren't that kosher. Never gave me the pleasure," Jacob said, smiling for real.

I was getting impatient. Enough with the schmoozing. "Did you put the hit on Dr. Joshua Lawrence at the Omshanti ashram in San Marcos?"

Now Avi actually *did* smile. "I was told by our research department that you had acquired some kind of new perceptive ability, Captain. But I wasn't certain you still held an allegiance for Israel. Do you both recognize and swear your allegiance to the State of Israel? Do you promise to never divulge anything that is said between us?"

We nodded our heads in agreement.

"We discovered key evidence at the scene of both of the murders of the IDF personnel. We checked the use of power during the time of the murders, and we noticed there were spikes in use. We traced the use to devices that had been connected to computers. We had no cameras in the room, but we were able to trace the digital record of our constant in-the-air drones that monitor any kind of computer or cell phone use. In each of these crime scenes, there was a record of extreme activity during the times the murders were committed."

"How did you link it to Dr. Lawrence?" I asked.

"The same way you trace any computer. Through his ISP number. It led directly to his home server at the Academic College at Yaffo. When we checked the school, we found that yes, there was a Dr. Joshua Lawrence working at the server's location. He was not a faculty member or an Israeli citizen. In fact, as we did more research into his phone and online records, we saw he had been in direct contact with Hamas and the Izz ad-Din al-Qassam Brigades. That's when we put in our top secret request to terminate to the Prime Minister."

"Oh, my God! Did you happen to find any record of business dealings between Lawrence and Hamas concerning sex trafficking?"

"How did you know? Yes, he was supplying young girls from the Omshanti ashrams directly to Hamas, who, in turn was selling them to ISIL and Boko Haram."

"We hate to spoil your party, Avi, but we think there might be another plan happening shortly. Two of Lawrence's advanced androids that were made in the likeness of my parents, Sid and Rose, are on their way to Israel. We don't know what they'll be doing, but if they can get here without being recorded, then maybe it also has something to do with Hamas." My mind was working as I glanced over Avi's sexual traumas. It looked like a secretary of his liked it in the tush, but I shut down my curiosity to focus on what was going down in the present.

"I have an idea. Could you check to see if there are any technology fairs or presentations to the government happening today or soon? The fact that Lawrence had dealings with the college in Tel Aviv, made me suspicious."

"Cohen! Get in here!" Avi yelled.

A short man in a parrot shirt stuck his head inside the door. "Sir?"

"Do a search for any technology companies or organizations giving presentations this week. Bring the list to me quickly."

"Right!"

After fifteen minutes, the same man appeared again. He handed a sheet of paper to his boss. "Today, in one hour, the Prime Minister will be viewing the final presentation of what the Serene implant can do to improve the health and medical treatment of IDF soldiers in the field under combat conditions. It's presented by the University of San Francisco and directly affiliated with the Defense Advanced Research Projects Agency. Can this be it?"

"DARPA my ass!" I said. "Dr. Watson, we need to get over there now."

"Right, Sherlock. Do you have your weapon?" Jacob asked.

I pulled out my Glock 19. All three of us smiled.

"I'm afraid we have to part company now," said Avi. "We can't be seen with other civilians. In fact, we'll be attending the presentation in separate vehicles. There will be some of your IDF soldiers around shortly to give you a ride over to the hotel."

"All right. We'll see you over there," I said.

CHAPTER EIGHTEEN: MASADA

Sid and Rose

The Grand Ballroom of the InterContinental David was filled with dignitaries from the Knesset, the IDF, and major universities. Sid and Rose were standing together on the stage along with a tall thin woman, their controller. All three wore dark suits, white shirts, and ties that bore the sky blue colors and the Israeli Stars of David.   Seated at the front row table were the contingent of the Office of Prime Minister. Akiva Fleischman, the current P.M., sat together with his Minister of the Interior Moshe Silver of the Likud party, and the Minister of Finance Yaron Roth of the Kulanu party.

Waiters weaved their balancing act trays between the dozens of tables with a variety of noshes, including bagels, cream cheese, pickled herring, smoked salmon, and mounds of fruit pastries. All eyes were watching the tall woman on stage. She had a stoic, dispassionate gaze. Her pale blue bug-eyes reminded the Prime Minister of Marty Feldman who played with Gene Wilder in *Young Frankenstein*, and he chuckled.

Sid and Rose had been present, over the years, when the private negotiations were conducted between the Prime Minister and their controller, Dr. Monica Farley. They had also been present when the two IDF soldiers—one male and one female—had their throats slit in the kosher manner by their controller. In fact, after they cleaned the room each time, Sid and Rose also traveled with Dr. Farley to the private meetings with Mr. Fleischman.

Their miraculous brains had recorded every second of these meetings, and several specific negotiations stood out. They were agreed upon by the P.M., which had now led to this final presentation at the Tel Aviv hotel. Sid was going over two of these dialogs in his computer brain:

'These androids are like stealth bombers, Mr. Prime Minister,' said Dr. Farley. 'One of the main features they have is the ability to condition the brain of a sleeping subject. The only way the human brain can be hacked is through the sense of smell. All other senses, including sight, sound, taste and touch, can be stopped by the brain's thalamus. But when these robots use odor, the smell goes directly to the subconscious, and it will provide a way for you to condition the sleeping person to perform actions that they are not consciously aware of. For example, perhaps you want your soldiers to refrain from using drugs or

alcohol. Sid and Rose would simply apply the odors of the booze and marijuana to the sleeping soldier and associate that odor with an electric shock.'

'I see! When the soldier brings the drink to his lips the smell will trigger the negative association,' the Prime Minister said.

'Quite right, sir. In fact, not to be flippant, but one could conceivably do the same thing by associating a noxious smell with a political candidate's voice, and a pleasing odor with another candidate's voice. When the subject was again awake he or she would respond favorably and vote for the candidate who had the voice associated with the pleasant smell.'

'I can see a lot of uses for this,' said Fleischman. 'And you say you'll be throwing this additional feature in with the main deal?'

'Yes, if you can get approval by next month,' said Dr. Farley.

Dr. Monica Farley walked to the center of the stage and stood there. Sid and Rose watched her with dispassionate stares. "Israel has become a beacon of religious hope and non-sectarian freedom because it creates a safe and secure land where terrorists are held at bay and the millions of sworn enemies who send barrage after barrage of missiles are thwarted by an Iron Dome of technology that can shoot down those missiles before they can kill Jewish civilians. Today, with the agreement between the government of Israel and our research and development team, we will demonstrate how 800 select troops have become upgraded by our unique Serene implant to take the place of the technology used in your Iron Dome battery installations all over Israel. Sid, please turn on the big screen LCD monitor."

The giant screen above the stage came on and it showed four different locations of Iron Dome batteries around Israel. One was in Gaza, another in Tel Aviv, one in Beersheba, and one in Jerusalem.

"As you'll see, these IAF soldiers have been implanted with our Serene devices, which can add to your arsenal of protection. We call this added defense ability 'David's Sling,' and it will shoot down short to medium-range rockets and ballistic missiles, guided projectiles, cruise missiles, aircraft and drones. Its range of coverage means it can destroy incoming threats over enemy territory, away from Israeli skies, and it is due to go operational in the coming year, thanks to your agreement. This system makes Israel the first country to actually bring The Singularity online for all the world to see. Your soldiers no longer will be limited by their biological brains and bodies. Instead, they will have the ability to plug into giant computers for instant computations, such as figuring out the best path to intercept enemy objects. In addition, your soldiers will be protected, 24/7, by the implants that monitor the soldier's health and mental well-being. The minute something goes wrong, the soldier can be taken offline and repaired or replaced, saving you millions of dollars."

There were many gasps and exclamations of approval from the audience.

"And, in the future, once approved by your government, you can actually replace these soldiers with our androids." Dr. Farley held out her arm toward Sid and Rose. "But first, let's see how these IAF soldiers can shoot down these drones we have hovering about 15,000 feet above each location."

On the screen, the IAF soldiers with the Serene implants went to work. They got on their laptops and calculated the coordinates of the flying drones. Then, they mentally signaled the missile batteries to fire off the batteries of rockets. The audience watched in rapt attention as the rockets swooped into the air and streaked toward their drone aircraft targets. When they struck, the drones ignited and exploded, sending shards of debris outward. The audience also exploded with cheers.

"Since 2006, more than 10,000 rockets and missiles were fired into Israel. Do you know another country that dealt with that many? Now, with our technology, Israel will be protected by technology that will make them the vanguard into the future of science all over the world."

Sid and Rose were scanning police activity with their brains. When they heard the conversation between Mossad agents, they immediately moved into evasive action. Dr. Farley received their warning signals through her implant.

Exactly ten minutes before the Mossad arrived at the InterContinental David Hotel, Dr. Monica Farley and her two androids were on their way by taxi to Mount Masada.

Rachel

The three IDF men who picked us up outside the Mossad headquarters in Tel Aviv were driving a Jeep. We expected to go speeding out to the hotel at the usual Israeli breakneck pace, but instead, the driver, a lean and dark young man of about nineteen, was driving at a moderate and safe speed down Rothschild Boulevard.

We were not surprised that they first confiscated our weapons, as the IDF are obsessive about not allowing civilians to be armed when they are in charge of things. They are that way with both Muslim and Jew. I always thought it was a bit paranoid, but don't get me started on the military.

They spoke to us in Hebrew, but I found their accents a bit strange. I knew that Bedouins served in the armed forces as a result of the agreement in 1948 when they helped Jews fight hostile Arabs. When I asked the driver if he were Bedouin, he nodded yes. I started perusing their sexual traumas with women in the West Bank, and that's when I knew these guys were certainly not nomads. They were Hamas members of the Izz ad-Din al-Qassam Brigades. Somehow, they had stolen IDF uniforms, ID, and the jeep.

Jacob was in the back seat with two of them, and I was in the front seat next to the driver. I didn't know how I could signal to my partner about the trap we were in, but this became a moot point when the short one in the back pulled out his handgun and held it on Jacob.

"Jew bastards!" said the short one. "Try to make a move and you die."

My shortness of breath was the first thing I noticed as we stepped out of the jeep and walked toward the Snake Path. As is usual in Israel, there were many soldiers, both in uniform and civilian clothes, who were walking around us. If only my brain had a way to send a message to them instead of this stupid trauma radar.

If my panic attacks had ever really subsided, they now began in earnest once more, as the thought of having to climb up this mountain, over a thousand feet to the top, filled my consciousness. My old dream took hold, and I kept thinking about the irony of being led up to the ancient fortress by our modern sworn enemy.

Jacob must have seen the look on my face because he turned toward me as we began the trek and took hold of my hand. "Rachel, you need to focus now. If we stand any chance, it will be through our attention to details."

"Quiet!" the tall soldier shouted. It was nine in the morning, so I knew they would not allow anybody else up after ten AM because of the desert heat. It took a little over an hour to scale this mountain. Each of the three Hamas operatives had an Uzi strapped around his shoulder. Their forged army identification must have been kosher because one of them was able to pay the 54 shekels for each of us to climb the mountain.

The clicking sound the rifles made as we climbed up the ever-winding dirt path irritated me no end. Why did they choose Masada? Did they know about my dream? I would hardly think it possible. I remembered what both Dr. Price and Guru Sharma told us about there being no coincidences. Even Dr. Jacob Stein would find all of this highly symbolic from a Jungian point of view.

If Mossad had already arrested Dr. Monica Farley, then maybe they'd be coming to the rescue. Otherwise, I thought this would be our last moments. As I watched Jacob's athletic calves tighten as he took bold strides up the mountain, I imagined him on top of me. Why hadn't we made love before all of this happened? Fate had not been on our side. This mystery had kept us locked in this obvious death march to oblivion. The salt pillars of the Dead Sea Valley stood out in the distance as we climbed higher. The endless blue sky above was forecasting a blistering hot day.

I suspected Farley was in on it with Lawrence. She certainly had the skills, and her access to all the financial records made her an important part of their plan. But what was their ultimate plan? Were they going to bug some of the technology they were selling to Israel? That had to be it. I wished I could have had a few more days to prove what their complete plan was, but this was probably the end. We were soon going to be blood spots on the desert floor.

When we reached the top of Masada, we filtered our way through the few tourists there. I could see most of them heading for the fortress where the ancient Jewish rebels held out against the Romans. That's also where most of them—except for two women and five children—took their lives. When I was in the IDF, we completed our Basic Training by running up the Snake Path to this fortress. We had a ceremony where we proclaimed "Masada shall not fall again!" Now that ceremony was held in Jerusalem at the Western Wall.

I kept trying to make faces at some of these people to show them we were in danger, but they just stared at me and then gave me some pretty ugly faces in response. We were walking toward the deserted end of the mountain top, where no tourists were. As a cost-saving measure, there were only two or three park rangers on duty, so nobody was following us. If we were pushed off this cliff, then maybe they'd find it prudent in the future to put in a camera or two or, god forbid, have a circling drone.

As we walked toward a precipice that had several boulders jutting out over the edge, I could see three figures standing in the shadows of the boulders. As we came closer, I could see who they were. It was Dr. Monica Farley from Omshanti, and my android parents, Sid and Rose.

Farley stepped out of the shadows to greet us. She had the same Morticia bug-eyed look wearing her black suit. The traumas about her having sex with the dogs made me suddenly quite sick to my stomach.

"Drs. Edelstein and Stein. You'll be unhappy to know that your friends, the Mossad, were unable to intervene. In fact, as you are probably aware by now, the technology package we negotiated with the Israeli Government to purchase has nothing to do with the murder of Dr. Lawrence or the murders of those hapless Jews. As far as the Prime Minister is concerned, Dr. Lawrence was the killer, but his work on these two robots and on our other projects at Omshanti were never compromised by his anti-Semitism."

"How can that be? You were certainly in on everything with him," I said.

"Only you know that. In actuality, I was the one who reported Dr. Lawrence and his anti-Semitic murders to the Mossad and to Prime Minister Fleischman directly. To them, I am a national hero. Omshanti does have legal affiliation with DARPA and many universities, including the University of San Francisco. Our technological credentials are impeccable, as far as they're concerned."

"Impeccably diabolical, you mean," said Jacob.

"Well, thank you for that compliment, Doctor. Now that you two fancy yourselves detectives, I would wager you know why you're up here." Farley motioned to the Hamas soldiers, and they moved us forward, with their pointed Uzi muzzles, until we stood about three feet from the edge of the cliff. My heart began to race.

Something inside made me want to collect all of my senses and become calm. I looked out over the cliff to the Dead Sea in the distance. So many stories were told about this land, and my mother, not an android, was the one who read them to me. I looked over at her robot self, and I smiled. She smiled back. My father was his usual stoic self. What was real and what was virtual? Did my serenity keep me from death right now?

"What is the big plan? Have you bugged the systems you're selling to the government?" I asked.

"Yes, I have just sold technology that will eventually take over the Israeli military. When it gets installed throughout the branches, we shall call upon our computer systems to begin Operation Armageddon. The world will think Israel began the war, but it will be our spyware that accomplished this feat. The nukes beneath the Negev will hit Iran, and the rest of the world will see Israel for what it is. A Zionist theological demagogue that keeps Palestinians as slaves and worships only money and power. If World War Three is unleashed, which we think is unlikely, then so be it. At any rate, Israel will be blamed for it all."

Since we were going to soon take a swan dive off Masada, I thought I would put my last word in. "Your technology isn't perfect. You are aware of that, right? When Dr. Lawrence implanted the SLIC in me, for example, he was unable to stop me from remembering what had occurred. In addition, instead of my becoming a Libertarian nymphomaniac, I was given the ability to see human sex traumas the way you watch video clips. By the way, you need to quit doing it doggie-style with your doggies, Monica, or you might start to bark."

If Farley were an android, I'm certain my joke would have fried her circuits. Instead, her eyes just bugged out more, and she actually raised her voice from the usual computer monotone level.

"Give two guns to the androids. I want her to see how well our technology can work."

The two Hamas soldiers unstrapped their Uzis, affixed two silencers to the barrels, and handed them to Sid and Rose.

"Sid and Rose, I order you to fire on these two Zionists!"

As my virtual father and mother raised their automatic weapons and pointed them at us, I began to see a blue and white light coming from each of them. The light was wavy at first, and then it began to form into human shapes and inanimate objects. I could see that what they were broadcasting before them were memories from my childhood. It was obvious that the brain scans that had been recorded and used as the platform for their mind circuits were now reacting in a strange way.

"Ready, aim, fire!" Farley yelled.

I closed my eyes, and I could hear the Dead Sea's waters calling me home. When the guns exploded in short bursts of rapid fire, I could feel nothing, so I opened my eyes.

Lying at the foot of the boulder were four bodies. Three were Hamas soldiers and one was Dr. Monica Farley.

I looked over at Dr. Jacob Stein, who was still standing to my right, and I smiled. It was starting to get very hot on top of Mount Masada, in many different ways.

EPILOGUE: BRIDE OF PASSION

Rachel

I've decided not to have my SLIC taken out. Since most crimes are committed during some kind of "passion," my ability to visually peruse the passionate recordings of suspects gives me quite an advantage. When we returned from Israel, my new private investigation partner, Dr. Jacob Stein, and I decided to go directly to Rabbi Miriam Price to get some advice.

The Israeli Government has obviously suspended any contracts made with Dr. Monica Farley and her laboratories. When the Hamas soldiers were identified, Prime Minister Fleischman ordered that special security measures be implemented on Mount Masada and all over Israel. Even though Guru Bhagwan Sharma has now vowed to hire all new scientists and research personnel for his Omshanti ashrams, I don't believe they'll be getting any government help any time soon.

Jacob and I have also learned a lesson about just where spiritual or unknown circumstances begin and scientific reality leaves off. This is why we've come to talk with our Jewish guru. She is now sitting across from us in her golem swing on the porch outside her home in La Jolla. This device is suspended from the porch awning by steel chains. It is colored red and blue, and it looks kind of like the Blob in that old Science Fiction movie, except this golem has a mouth with a red tongue sticking out of it.

"It was quite fantastic, Rabbi," I said, holding Jacob's hand. We were sitting in more conventional Israeli blue lounge chairs that had *tzitzit* hanging on the sides like the strings on a Jewish prayer shawl. "My android parents were unable to fire the guns. We've asked scientists, and they can't offer any explanation as to why these machines would change targets like that. However, since these particular robots were using human brain scans, we thought maybe there may have been some emotional component that transferred into the processing unit of each android."

"In other words, when Rachel saw the memories from her childhood being projected in front of her parents' bodies, these androids must have been connecting her physical image with the images from their scanned memories," said Jacob.

"I can only speculate about what this may mean in terms of the Kabbalah. Because all light, and therefore all atoms, come from the Creator in the form of Ein Sof, then there's no reason why their memories wouldn't be associated with family love. How can any parent—even one who owns the virtual identity of parenthood—kill his or her own child? If God intervened between Abraham's slaying of his son, Isaac, perhaps it was God who also intervened in this instance."

We continued to discuss how my implant was working for me, and how I was able to first suspect Dr. Lawrence and then Dr. Farley and connect them with the sex trafficking. I explained how profiteering from sex tourism came up during my PTSD therapy session with the first murder victim, Sergeant Seth Berman. I then realized that the only way the crime scenes could have been cleansed was to have robots do the job. This, again, pointed to Dr. Lawrence. In addition, Lawrence murdered our Kabbalah discussion member and IDF vet, Dan Rosen. The old couple who escorted him out of the temple's bingo games must have been the Sid and Rose androids made up to be elderly folks.

"The real breakthrough in the case came when the Mossad told us they were the ones who put the hit on Dr. Lawrence. I looked around and saw that Dr. Monica Farley had disappeared from the ashram. I knew she would be in Israel working through the Academic College in Tel Aviv." It was quite horrendous how terrorists were able to use academic and religious communities as fronts to exploit their madness around the world.

"Guru Sharma must have been marked for destruction after the connection with the terrorists was discovered," said Jacob.

"Even if the robots of my parents had killed us, I believe Dr. Farley's scheme would have eventually come apart. The Mossad already knew a lot about her from us, and I'm certain they would have found more evidence." I stood up and pulled Jacob up with me. I wanted to get out to the ashram before sundown.

"You must remember that in these days of world terror the totalitarians will use our freedoms against us. Only the *Ein Sof* can keep you safe," the Rabbi pointed out, standing up with us.

When we hugged her and kissed her cheeks at the door, she gazed over our shoulders at the sun. "Paradise on Earth will soon come to pass. We have wonderful Kabbalah practitioners like you to make it a real possibility," she said.

* * *

"I guess our martyrdom will have to wait," Jacob smiled. We were inside Guru Sharma's Bride of Passion Chamber.

I was now in my thirties, not thirteen, so as I lay on top of the strewn rose petals, my heavier weight made the water bed undulate quite a bit more. "Watch it, lover boy. We don't want to get seasick on here," I told Jacob as he crawled onto the bed looking like a panther on the prowl. His Michael Douglas smile was in full display, as was his erection quite a bit below it.

My body's passion points began to pulsate vigorously, and I was quite aroused— something I had never experienced before. As Jacob began to place his warm, aromatic and slippery hands on my body, I shivered with joyous abandon. When his right hand reached up to caress my right ear, I began to pant.

When the explosions boomed, we both reacted with immediate speed. We threw on our robes and ran from the passion chamber and out of the temple.

Outside, in the quad, all of the buildings were ablaze. Hundreds of devotees were screaming and running from the collapsing buildings. All of the buildings had been struck by missiles from two drone aircraft that were circling above us.

Linda came screaming from the Genetics Lab. "Guru is dead! He was hit directly when the bomb struck the lab."

A loudspeaker began to broadcast a voice from one of the large drones:

> *I have enjoyed round one in our joust. Detectives, we shall meet again very soon. In fact, I can give you a single clue to put you on your guard. Remember the LBGTQ community? Since you defamed the Maithuna, my next puzzle will involve the 'q' in that acronym. Queer means strange, does it not? Also, it means someone who has not decided to which sexual identity he or she wants to adhere.*
>
> *Therefore, I will present you with a case involving a queer event. I want to commend you on your first case. You were quite a challenge. However, I have no use for what is left behind. Make no mistake. I will be continuing my science and research, and you will be feeling my genius inventions in most personal ways!*
>
> *The Intergalactic Convergence will still happen, but not with imposters like Bhagwan Sharma. Once I have purged the world, and had my fun with you, I will then begin the final transference.*
>
> *Shalom!*

Jacob and I watched as the drones began to rise up into the San Marcos skies. We could hear the sirens in the near distance, and we had to get outside the compound before the smoke engulfed us. As we ran toward the exit, which was not yet on fire, I kept thinking about Guru Sharma and his spiritual presence. All of the fantastic technology and breakthrough devices, including my android parents, were now destroyed. In my tradition, however, and in most spiritually advanced religions, it was survival that mattered in the long run.

We had survived to fight another day, and I knew the coming days, weeks and months were going to be the most challenging of my life. I still have my serene outlook on life that the Kabbalah practice infused inside me. No matter what trials I experience, I can always return to the Tree of Life and the Tree of Knowledge to begin again. Just as God's eternal vigilance keeps these trees changing to survive the storms and the natural tribulations, so too can I collect myself again to be able to withstand my own psychological unrest and create a safe home for others to enjoy.

Jacob moved toward me as I stood alone thinking about all these things. I reached out with my flesh-covered branch and brought him into the shade of my reincarnation. I wanted to finish our dalliance with Tantric passion. It's the least we could do to pay tribute to Guru Sharma and his ashram of ash.

* * *

Inside Temple Emanuel, Rabbi Miriam Price was moving her pale hands deftly over the touchscreen LED computer. As she dragged the image of the drone across the map toward its rendezvous with the cell members hiding in the hills of San Marcos, her other hand was enlarging the frame of the live video that had been taken by the drone during its attack on the ashram. When she used this remote control technology, she felt in her heart and soul that she was manipulating the magical forces of the Kabbalah—the tradition that had been passed down over the thousands of years and was now under her control.

Rabbi Price now had accumulated the technology she needed to establish what she knew would be Paradise on Earth. All of the prototypes from the Omshanti labs had been copied from the databases, and all of the blueprints for the new inventions were safe and secure inside her private underground cells around the world. The inevitable scourge of criminals like Lawrence and Farley were bound to happen. They were hired to carry out her goals, and their methods were greedy and dangerous, so they were discovered. Rabbi Price would be making certain that her next foray into the "queer world" of political correctness would not have such sloppy executioners.

She wanted to entertain herself by toying with the orphan, Rachel Edelstein, who was finally able to figure out the elaborate threads of secrecy leading to their plot against Israel. But she hadn't deduced the Rabbi's role in this conspiracy. Rabbi Price believed Israel had wandered away from the ancient tradition of the Kabbalah, and it was now headed toward destruction. The *Shekinah* was never meant to be a single nation or state. It was meant to be the female-controlled Paradise on Earth where men and their horrific weapons of total annihilation could be rendered forever impotent.

Rabbi Price wrapped her blue prayer shawl or tallit around her shoulders and picked-up the tefillin, or small boxes containing the scrolls with verses from the Torah, which were bound with leather straps. She then began to tie the first strap around her head so that the box was protruding from her forehead and then she wrapped the other one around her arm seven times. Finally, in order to make the total sacrilege complete, she began to daven, her reddish-brown hair falling onto the computer screen as she leaned forward, praying out loud in Hebrew the same curse that was previously used on the former liberal Prime Minister Yitzhak Rabin. The Pulsa diNura.

The curse she chanted was placed upon the current PM, Akiva Fleischman: "Angels of destruction will hit him. He is damned wherever he goes. His soul will instantly leave his body... and he will not survive a month. Dark will be his path and God's angel will chase him. A disaster he has never experienced will befall him and all curses known in the Torah will apply to him. I deliver to you, the angels of wrath and ire, Akiva, the son of Leila Fleischman, that you may smother him and the specter of him, and cast him into hell, and dry up his wealth, and plague his thoughts, and scatter his mind that he may be steadily diminished until he reaches his death. Put to death the cursed Akiva. May he be damned, damned, damned!"

ABOUT THE AUTHOR

Jim Musgrave's work has been featured in *Best New Writing 2011*, Hopewell Press, Titusville, N.J. He won First Place in the Chanticleer CLUE competition for Best Historical Mystery, and he was a semi-finalist in the Black River Chapbook Competition and finalist in the Heekin Scholarship Award for Creative Writing, Finalist Next Generation Book Awards and Global eBook Awards. He was also in a Bram Stoker Award Finalist volume of horror fiction, *Beneath the Surface, 13 Shocking Tales of Terror*, Shroud Publishing, San Francisco, CA. His short story, "Zeru," was published in *Mixer*. He has also published six novels and three collections of short stories at EMRE Publishing, LLC. His complete Historical Steampunk Mystery series starring Detective Pat O'Malley, is featured around the U. S. library system under the Self-E collection. He is owner of EMRE Publishing, LLC, and he created the only mobile application platform that allows the author to create, market and sell multimedia eBooks through the Embellisher™ Mobile Publishing system. He taught at Caltech and in the San Diego Community Colleges in San Diego where he presently lives with his wife Ellen.